THE LE

Series Titles

What Makes You Think You're Supposed to Feel Better
Jody Hobbs Hesler

Fugitive Daydreams
Leah McCormack

The Effects of Urban Renewal on Mid-Century America and Other Crime Stories
Jeff Esterholm

Hoist House: A Novella & Stories
Jenny Robertson

Finding the Bones: Stories & A Novella
Nikki Kallio

Self-Defense
Corey Mertes

Where Are Your People From?
James B. De Monte

Sometimes Creek
Steve Fox

The Plagues
Joe Baumann

The Clayfields
Elise Gregory

Kind of Blue
Christopher Chambers

Evangelina Everyday
Dawn Burns

Township
Jamie Lyn Smith

Responsible Adults
Patricia Ann McNair

Great Escapes from Detroit
Joseph O'Malley

Nothing to Lose
Kim Suhr

The Appointed Hour
Susanne Davis

Praise for
What Makes You Think You're Supposed to Feel Better

"Jody Hobbs Hesler is the writer who reminded me why I love short stories. Whether writing about a young mother-to-be and the fortune-teller next door, or a man who buys a giant M&M advertisement for his grown daughter, or a woman's fascination with her dead neighbor's house, Hobbs Hesler unerringly finds the spaces between people, or in between the self and its desires, and probes those places, often with great subtlety and restraint, occasionally with gleeful absurdity and wit. Her characters are fundamentally decent people trying to do better in a world that constrains them through place and circumstance. Their struggles reveal their natural compassion and sensitivity and—surging through now and again like a consuming flame—the primal needs of the self. This is a collection to be treasured, returned to, and remembered as a source of revelation."

—Pamela Petro
author of *The Long Field*

"Hobbs Hesler's debut story collection is closely set geographically in and around Charlottesville, Virginia, over the past fifty years—not the academic's nor the tourist's Charlottesville, but working-class neighborhoods, convenience stores, motels. The author has a keen eye and ear and the voices of her aspirant, wounded, and wounding characters—men, women, children—ring true. The territory here is an uneven playing field, but heart ache, heart break, betrayal and failure are the common, levelling experiences. Hobbs Hesler creates her characters and their world with clarity and respect, a deceptively simple style graced by brilliant detail and dialogue."

—Ellen Prentiss Campbell
author of *Frieda's Song* and *The Bowl with Gold Seams*

"Jody Hobbs Hesler's stories are perfect nuggets of observation, artful and spare at once. Ordinary lives are pierced by disappointment, happiness and grace lost and found; her characters' emotions are described with such love and precision that the reader cannot fail to empathize with them despite, or perhaps because of, their flaws. This is a collection that brings you in and takes you with it; every story is so deeply felt."

—Louise Marburg
author of *No Diving Allowed* and *You Have Reached Your Destination*

"Jody Hobbs Hesler's stories in *What Makes You Think You're Supposed to Feel Better* are just as likely to strike a tender note as to twist the knife as she illuminates the human flaws we all have. Deeply relatable for anyone who has struggled to make their way through life, Hobbs Hesler poses questions of how to handle heartbreak while still offering ideas about salvation. There is a tension in this collection: we never know when something will turn to the better or toward the worse. What ties the book together is a deep sense of longing, whether it is for safety, stability, comfort, or love. We know these people because we are them. A memorable debut."

—Wendy J. Fox
author of *What If We Were Somewhere Else* and *If The Ice Had Held*

"An unflinching inquiry into the psyche of small-town America, Jody Hobbs Hesler's debut story collection, *What Makes You Think You're Supposed to Feel Better*, lays bare the secret fears and yearnings we hold close to our chests, asking how well we can ever know those people closest to us, and how well we can ever know ourselves. Hobbs Hesler's prose is sharp and precise, her characters fully formed, and her endings so delicately crafted, they leave you with a sense of having grasped something vital about the human condition."

—Elizabeth Shick
author of *The Golden Land*

"Hobbs Hesler writes stories that are disarming in their simplicity yet devastating in their tenderness. Her characters are everyday folk, and yet as they traverse their ostensibly average lives, in average neighborhoods, Hobbs Hesler manages to tease out the moral conflicts which sit at the heart of what it means to be a human in relationship with another human. It's difficult to say who's the hero and who's the anti-hero in these stories. All we know is that each character loves and wants and aches for a connection which is quite often elusive. In this way, Hobbs Hesler has crafted such a facsimile of real life that you will shed real tears and, after the last page, look at your neighbors with a softened gaze."

—Celeste Mohammed
author of *Pleasantview*

"You'll find beautifully realized characters in this lovely collection. These are people you'll recognize from town, from a time when you took the kids to the boss's house for a pool party, and there was the creepy neighbor across the street, and the fortune teller on the next block, and the kids were in summer camp, recognizable people in circumstances that are so clearly delivered they will feel like personal experience, like memory— and the whole journey through takes on a pleasurable tinge of nostalgia: It's all there in Jody Hobbs Hesler's prose magic."

—Lisa Cupolo
author of *Have Mercy On Us*
W.S. Porter Prize winner

What Makes You Think You're Supposed to Feel Better

stories

Jody Hobbs Hesler

Cornerstone Press
Stevens Point, Wisconsin

Cornerstone Press, Stevens Point, Wisconsin 54481
Copyright © 2023 Jody Hobbs Hesler
www.uwsp.edu/cornerstone

Printed in the United States of America by
Point Print and Design Studio, Stevens Point, Wisconsin

Library of Congress Control Number: 2023938628
ISBN: 978-1-960329-07-3

This is a work of fiction. Names, characters, businesses, places, events, and incidents
are either the products of the author's imagination or used in a fictitious manner. Any
resemblance to actual persons, living or dead, or actual events is purely coincidental.

Cornerstone Press titles are produced in courses and internships offered by the
Department of English at the University of Wisconsin–Stevens Point.

DIRECTOR & PUBLISHER   EXECUTIVE EDITOR
Dr. Ross K. Tangedal   Jeff Snowbarger

SENIOR EDITORS
Lexie Neeley, Monica Swinick, Kala Buttke

PRESS STAFF
Carolyn Czerwinski, Grace Dahl, Zoie Dinehart, Kirsten Faulkner, Hannah Fenrick,
Angela Green, Brett Hill, Ryan Jensen, Kenzie Kierstyn, Eli Masini, Maddy Mauthe,
Maggie Payson, Natalie Reiter, Lauren Rudesill, Maria Scherer, Arianna Soto, Cat
Scheinost, Anthony Thiel, Chloe Verhelst, Abbi Wasielewski

For my family, with love and gratitude

Stories

I can't describe
what it's like to
sit on opposite ends
of a park bench and
not know how
to get any closer

—Kenyatta Rogers

Alone

The cure for loneliness is solitude.
—Marianne Moore

It hit the papers the second morning after they found him, all about Beane's body, forgotten and rotting in the house directly across the street from mine. Suicide. According to the article, a fellow gamer half a country away in the Midwest noticed Beane wasn't showing up on his live feed. Swore there was an eerie cast to the light around his empty chair, like death had changed the color of the room. After two weeks, he finally figured out how to contact authorities.

This was the summer that Nola, our next-door neighbor, got a goat named Mr. Biscuit and started raising chickens. Will and I were happy about the easy promise of fresh eggs, but we worried the animal pens in her backyard would reek in the heat. The first day we noticed the smell, we figured that's where it was coming from.

It was the middle of a particularly hot spell, even for a Virginia summer, so of course the smell got worse each day. Ali from three doors down guessed it was baking trash. Dean insisted it must be a decaying deer tangled in the kudzu down by the train tracks. None of us thought of Beane.

We didn't think of him because we never saw him, and Beane liked it that way. He never poked a head out during neighborhood parties, rarely came outside at all, and when he did, he was posterboard pale with a frothy beard that hung down to his chest. A Schwan's truck delivered food to his house a couple times a month. Whenever it came onto the street, Ella begged us for a dollar and raced to the door, thinking it was the ice cream man.

Probably the longest conversation any of us had with him was mine, not long after we moved onto the street. It must have been a trash day, because Beane sightings most commonly happened around bringing trash cans to or from the curb. I introduced myself and told him how I was a medical illustrator and worked from home. That was back before Lynn was born, when Ella was still a toddler. Beane told me he was a livestream gamer and worked from home too.

"I expect we'll be seeing a lot of each other then," I said.

"I doubt it," Beane said, with a smile that made it seem like his solitude was a trick he was playing on the world. He explained how most gamers kept unusual hours and lots more lived in Europe and Asia in altogether different time zones anyway. I wondered what such a solitary existence would feel like, but I could tell from Beane's wry grin that he had no answering curiosity about me.

"I'm nocturnal," he added, almost joyfully.

The same day as the newspaper article, a professional cleaning company came in a huge white van. We gathered on the street to watch. A generator rattled and bellowed all day. Hoses of different sorts extended from the van and into the house. We figured it was the same kind of company the mafia might use. Or people cleaning up after Katrina. Or after an Ebola outbreak. The cleaners carried out what must have been some of Beane's furniture, draped in white plastic, and hauled it away with them when they left.

"Can't sleep?" I asked Will that night. Standing at our bedroom window, I could hear him behind me, rolling, restless. I was peering at Beane's house through the slats of the blinds. Storm-blown leaves from the summer banked in his gutters, and acorns dropped, thudded, and rolled to join them. Everything pinkish in the streetlight.

"We should have invited him around," Will said.

"Beane?"

"Maybe he told funny jokes? Played banjo? Maybe we could've played some chess." Will rubbed his eyes and hiked up on one elbow. His movement rustled the sheets. "All those parties we had, right outside his window."

Parties on our street invariably wound up dribbling into our yard, with people crossing into Beane's without thinking of it. Our yard joined Beane's at the cul-de-sac and they rolled together toward the train tracks. Kids could run around without worrying about cars. Everyone else on the street was like us, with newborns and toddlers. No one else was like Beane.

"He could've come out. Nobody stopped him."

"Nobody asked him," Will said.

Streetlight shot in through the blinds, throwing pink bars onto the carpet and brightening our bedroom to a sickish shade. "Maybe he didn't want us to."

Sometimes during a party, with Ella crawling wild and muddy across my lap and Lynn nearby threatening to nurse yet again, I would gaze up at Beane's front window, which forever flickered in shifting TV light, and I'd fantasize about slipping into his house, invisible, to see what it felt like on the other side of so much human noise.

"Come back to bed," Will said. He lowered onto his side and flung the sheet back up around his shoulders.

The blinds clapped together behind me, and we settled against each other again. "You don't even play chess," I said. His breath heavied and I slithered beyond his reach, seeking my own cool space in the sheets.

The cleaning company was thorough, and the only smells leftover were summer ones. Hot dry grass. Sweaty children. Honeysuckle blooming among the kudzu. Even by the end of the next week we were back to doing the things we'd been doing before. The kids ate and slept and played. We worked and cooked and folded laundry. Whenever a train would clack down the track, Nola would show up with a trail of her kids and Mr. Biscuit, and I would show up with Lynn clamped to my hip and Ella grasping my hand. We'd stand on the grassy rise by the tracks, waving at the passing cars like always.

And whenever the ice cream man came, Ella would run out with her dollar. The next time the Schwan's truck pulled up, a dollar wilted from her fingers while we watched the driver park, halt at the line of police tape across Beane's walk, then look up in wonder before driving away again, with all of Beane's food still inside.

The tail end of July and most of August passed this way. A few trees showed their first yellow leaves. Police took down the tape, and the first day of school rolled around.

Like a lot of us, our oldest was starting kindergarten, so this was our first ever first day of school. Some on the street had younger kids, like Nola's brood, or babies like Lynn, but none had older kids. Regular school started earlier and lasted longer than preschool had, and none of us were used to the early hour at the bus stop or the prospect of such a long day for our kids.

The morning air was thick and muggy, the sky listless late-August white. Nola still wore slippers and nibbled an edge of toast. A headband pressed her looping curls in place. Most of us held cups of coffee. Dean and his husband had thought to ice theirs and the rest of us were jealous.

The kids stood in line clutching lunch boxes, looking tidier than usual. Two ladybug barrettes fastened Ella's fine thin hair at her ears. Nola's Esther stood straighter than ever and wore a white dress sprayed with flowers. Mr. Biscuit nudged at her lunchbox.

When the bus came, it creaked and throttled and took them away. "Can you believe it?" we asked each other. "How did they get that old." We watched the bus turn the corner and grind through its gears out of sight. We had tears in our eyes.

After Lynn's morning nap, I brought her to Nola's backyard like any other day. Ali brought baby Brent and we sat under the trees. After Lynn nursed, the grownups shared our ritual cup of coffee, and Mr. Biscuit chased the chickens and Nola's two-year-old Joey around the yard. The heat of the day began to press down.

"Do you ever get lonely?" I asked them.

They laughed. Nola waved her hand at the display of children and farm animals. "I'm never alone," she said.

"That's not the same thing."

"You'll get used to it," Ali said, patting my arm with his free hand, assuming our two-hour trial run of a school morning had hit me harder than him.

At my drafting table later, I faced a troop of fine-pointed colored pencils and a photograph to sketch for my next assignment, a cadaver's sliced open chest cavity. While I worked, I rocked Lynn in her seat with my foot.

Without Ella, I had to entertain her myself. She got fussy. She didn't want tummy time on the floor. She rejected the soft toys I dangled over her. She wanted to nurse again as soon as she finished. I forgot all about my own lunch until my stomach clenched and gurgled. I had just enough time to throw a sandwich together before Will arrived home. He planned to come home early enough to meet the bus with me every day this first week.

Lexa was on a late-night rotation for her surgical residency so she could meet the afternoon bus too, and Dean and Ali were also there. The sun was hot.

"What if it doesn't come back?" I asked. Lynn, sweaty and warm, thrashed in my arms.

"What else would it do?" Lexa said.

Ali patted my arm again. Mr. Biscuit bleated at the flash of yellow, just now coming into view.

In bed that night, Will and I listened to soft rain tapping the roof. Thunder trembled in the distance. We hoped it wouldn't turn into a full-fledged storm and wake Ella. By bedtime, purple rings drooped under her eyes from her long day. I asked Will if he ever got lonely.

"Who has time?" he said, rubbing a calloused palm against my bare shoulder. Lightning flashed white blades through the blinds. Thunder wobbled from one end of the sky to the other. "If I was lonely," he said, "I'd just come home and be with you and Ella."

"What if that didn't work?"

"It always has."

More blades at the window, then a clap of thunder so quick and close I jumped.

———

It was after Ella went to school the next day that I started to smell that smell again, only a figment of what it had been. I had a deadline to meet, so Will came home extra early and took Lynn for a long run in the jogging stroller. At my desk, I sketched a pulmonary valve. I couldn't remember the last time I had been alone.

At first, the smell seemed to be coming from downstairs. When I got downstairs, it seemed to be coming from outside. When I got outside, it seemed to be coming from every direction, but so soft it was hard to track.

In Beane's yard, holes from the posts where police had draped their tape still gouged the ground. The earth looked fresh and fertile there, wet from last night's rain. Beane's lawn was growing tall and weedy. I didn't remember him or anyone cutting his grass, but it was always short. Some of the neighbors hired services, so guys dragged enormous mowers all around the block, making a ruckus and waking sleeping babies. Beane must have hired out, but it seemed strange to forget already. I wondered how they knew not to come anymore.

His mailbox hung beside his front door, empty, so either the police had told the post office or Beane had relatives somewhere calling in directions from afar. I wondered if realtors would have to tell their clients what had happened here when the house went up for sale.

I edged down from Beane's front stoop and slunk along behind his bushes there, peeking into windows. Vacant spaces replaced furniture the cleaning guys had taken. Beane must not have had much to begin with because hardly anything was left. A framed poster of the Empire State Building on one wall. A lounge chair. A coffee table.

The smell wasn't coming from out here, but a hint of it drifted in the air. I walked around the back of Beane's house, opening the gate of his waist-high chain link fence to let myself in. It was a big yard and a good fence. He could have kept a dog back here. I bet he never wanted one, though. If I lived by myself, I wouldn't want a dog either. Then you wouldn't be alone.

I tried Beane's backdoor. It was locked. I checked the basement windows. Also locked. I peeked under the back-door mat. It was soggy from last night's rain. The key was cool and moist. I slipped it into the deadbolt. I had to jimmy it, but it turned.

Inside, the air was antiseptic, like a hospital, and stuffy. Way underneath was the smell. What I must have picked up from across the street. Some vestige of the original clinging to the floorboards, maybe, or to the paint on the walls, or the plaster of the ceilings. It was faint, but it was everywhere.

Images of decay arrived from memory in the form of high color contrast medical illustrations. Body fluids leaking. Shades of orange, yellow, and mud brown. Eyes bulging. Red, white, midnight purple. Skin giving way. Ash, blue-black, bright bone white.

The paper said they found Beane sitting in a chair, so surely the cleaners heaved that one into the dump. From the lounge chair they left behind, you could see straight across to my house. I reclined, flicked the handle to pop the footrest up.

If people were inside our house, you wouldn't see much detail, but you could watch them like TV. You would know when they were there, moving around, speaking to each other. You would know when they laughed. When they shouted. When they cried.

The chair was comfortable. I felt my arms sink into the armrests, my legs into the seat. The corduroy in faded taupe had softened from years of use, with patches at the ends of the armrests where the cord had all but worn away.

I watched from the chair when Nola bounded up my porch steps and knocked at my screen door. I hadn't planned to be gone long, so I had left the front door swung wide. Mr. Biscuit bobbed onto the porch, and Nola screeched the screen door open. From Beane's chair, I could hear her call for me. She stepped inside.

When Mr. Biscuit butted the screen door, I could hear the soft rap of his head. Nola came back outside, pulled the front door closed behind her, and looked in every direction. But not toward Beane's house.

Later, Will trotted back into the yard with the jogging stroller. He unloaded a sleepy Lynn and disappeared inside with her. Soon he reemerged from the front door and stood on the porch, calling my name. It must be time for the bus. Lynn would want to nurse soon. That pulmonary valve sat unfinished on my desk. I must have been sitting in Beane's house, in Beane's chair, in the soft fug of that awful smell, for over an hour.

But it didn't feel awful. It didn't feel awful when I saw Will lean his head out our front door again. He turned every direction, except toward Beane's house, looking and calling my name. It didn't feel awful when I watched him leave for the bus stop with Lynn strapped to his chest or when he returned holding Ella's hand. I could tell from the way Ella's head moved that she was talking and excited, but I couldn't hear what she said. Will was louder, saying things like, "Oh really?" Even from the muted sound of his voice, I could tell he was worried.

That didn't feel awful either. It should have, but it didn't.

I got hungry. I had to use the bathroom. My breasts ached with milk. By now, Will must have given Lynn a bottle. But I didn't move from the chair. I watched a few leaves spiral from trees in the wind. Listened to the thonk of acorns on Beane's roof, the scrabble of squirrel claws, the clatter of the train. Birds swooped and chirped outside.

Will wouldn't understand. I knew that much before I saw Nola at my front door, without Mr. Biscuit, before I heard her coo something to Ella and saw her disappear inside so Will could leave. Before I watched him circle around our house in wider and wider arcs. Looking. Calling. I could feel his animal heartbeat as if I were inside his skin.

He wouldn't understand, so it was time to leave. I cranked the chair forward, tucked its footrest and gave one last look around the sterile, empty space. I etched the feeling, the blankness, the freedom of it, deep into the back of my mind. Then I stood up, retraced my steps out of the house, relocked the backdoor, re-hid the key, re-clasped the chain link gate, and walked away, one slow footfall at a time, leaving the smell behind, along with Beane's looted home.

Wading again through the reedy grass, I made my way back to the cul-de-sac, where Will was disappearing around the corner, a flash of white in the early dusk that powdered the sky in dusty purples and pinks.

"Will?"

When he turned and saw me standing where I had not been moments before, his face registered the shock of someone witnessing a person rise from the dead. Seeing a ghost, or something like it, you don't run at first. You hold still. You have no idea what to do.

"Pearl?" His voice quavered. "Are you okay? What happened?"

Slowly, we walked toward each other until we met in the middle of our street. I rested a hand on his arm. "It's okay. I just needed to be alone for a while. I lost track of time." I gave him a soft smile and studied his face as the pressure of my touch gradually eased his worry. Still, a question flickered in his eyes, and I was conscious of a scent, lingering in my hair or on my clothes, of a hospital room, maybe, and a trace of rot.

"Let's go home," I said. Will followed me back to our house.

Inside, Nola was putting dirty dishes into the dishwasher from the meal she had fed Ella. She had bathed the girls and put them to bed for us too.

"She was out for a walk," Will explained, though I'd never said so. "She lost track of time."

Nola looked unconvinced, or suspicious, and I could feel the caution of her silence. When she needed to leave, Will walked her to our backdoor and thanked her again. I overheard her whispering something to him about fevers and dehydration. Back in the kitchen, Will offered me juice, a sandwich, anything I might want.

"I just want a bath," I said. I filled our tub with scalding water and added drops of lavender oil, let the floral fumes fill the room, then sank my naked flesh into them. I basked in the heat and the scent. I wanted this scent to replace the other one.

Lynn screamed awake and broke the silence. My body now smelled of nothing but flowers, and I pulled the drain and let bathwater drip away. I unhooked my bathrobe from the back of the door and wrapped myself in it. Ella woke too, and I heard Will's quiet voice comforting her, asking for her help with Lynn, the way he always did, to include her in our attentions to the baby.

In the hallway, Will cradled the bawling Lynn in his arms. Ella beamed at the sight of me and slipped a hand into mine.

"Come on," Will said to Ella. "We can all sleep together in the big bed tonight."

We tumbled onto the bed then, Ella giggling, Lynn beginning to pitch into her loudest keening, Will making room for everyone and fixing all the covers. Lynn nursed away the painful tension of my overfull breasts, and I relaxed against the headboard. Ella curled into my thigh with Will shelled around her, draping a hand across her and my lap. We were one unit, the four of us. Everyone attached. My bath oil mingled with Ella's freshly shampooed hair, Lynn's clean milkiness, Will's soap and sweat. Their breathing found a rhythm together, and my breath caught with the wonder of it.

Then kept catching. Eyes closed, I imagined myself back into Beane's empty house. A hollow wind rushed around me. I opened my mouth and gulped at the air until my breath came easy again.

Sweetness

Me and Vern and Alfred arrived at the same time with our parents and little brothers and sisters. Our Moms wore waterproof lipstick and swimsuits under their sundresses. Our Dads swapped their usual grease-stained old jeans and liquor ad t-shirts for polos and khaki shorts from the backs of their dresser drawers. Before we went in, our dads took turns lecturing us on how to behave—please, thank you, yessir, no sir, no curse words, and for God's sake don't drop your phones in the pool—because you can't be yourself at the boss's house.

Mr. Wilkinson just got promoted to regional manager and was throwing pool parties for all the linemen that worked for him now. I'd never been to a boss's house before, and I was pretty sure Vern and Alfred hadn't either. Everything here was better than us, down to the tan and white pebbles of the half-mile long driveway that led up past their swimming pool to their shining glass house. Our houses had rutted dirt drives, broken gutters, and paintstripped front doors.

We knew Mr. Wilkinson's daughter Juliet from school. The rest of the guys only knew her by sight, but I'd been in art class with her the year before last, our last year of middle school. Still, she was too smart and pretty and rich to act like she knew any of us back.

Before we stepped through the bushes toward the pool, Vern whispered, "Bet she looks hot as hell in a swimsuit."

15

Vern talked about girls a lot more than he talked to them. Juliet was gorgeous—all the right proportions and pretty hair and wide-open eyes. You wanted to rest your hands on every curve, taste her lips with yours, but, for years before she even was one, she acted exactly like you'd expect a boss's daughter would. She might turn her head in our direction when we were laughing about something in the cafeteria and shoot us a look that could level the feelings right out of us. Make us forget what was funny. Forget anything ever had been funny.

We tiptoed barefoot onto the sunbaked slates around the pool, our shoes hanging from our hands. The slates ended at a vine-strung stone wall behind the diving board. Back there, a stainless-steel grill, big as half a car, flared in the sunlight. A whole little outdoor kitchen surrounded it, complete with gleaming cupboards and a mini fridge. Huge pots of ferny trees seemed to thumbtack the pool in place. Living at their house was probably like a pool party every day.

Juliet sat in one of the reclining chairs, wearing a man's button-down shirt with the sleeves rolled up and cutoff jeans gouged with rips. She noticed us waiting in line as our moms and dads shook her dad's hand, jostling one foot to the other on the slates to keep from burning ourselves. We were the only kids here her age, but, same as at school, she looked away from us, scanning the mountains that rose up behind her house, tugging at the threads of her cutoffs, canceling us out.

Mr. Wilkinson ended up shaking everybody's hands hello, even our little brothers' and sisters'. Mrs. Wilkinson started handing around iced tea. She was younger than our moms with a perfect tan and fingernails painted like pink pearls. We couldn't help eyeing how tightly her dress hugged her chest, the slit of her cleavage right in front of our faces as she pressed glasses slicked with ice sweat into our hands. Juliet watched us watching her and razored her lips into a thin line.

Mr. Wilkinson yanked beers out of his shiny mini fridge to toss to our dads. They caught the cans in both hands and pretended they were used to bosses palling around with them. But really they were more natural scaling poles thirty, forty feet in the air and wrestling with live wires.

"Well, get comfortable!" Mrs. Wilkinson spoke like a substitute teacher trying to make us like her, while we stood around wondering, should we finish our tea first? Or cannonball right in like the little kids who got here before us? Or wait for some signal from Juliet? Vern's little brother took a running start and splashed full speed into the deep end beside us, spraying us with icy beads of chlorine water, and Alfred's sister pin-dropped in right after him.

The little kids splashed around the shallow end or rotated in bright animal-shaped floats. We sat there watching them, letting sweat drizzle down our necks and missing those days when we goofed off without thinking about it first.

Sitting there feeling dorky and stuck, I flashed back through art class memories for something I could walk over and talk about with Juliet. I pictured myself, like a teen rom com hero, the way they swagger and hold their bodies like they know what to do with them. The only story that came to me, though, was from the time we wound up alone in the kiln closet when I caught her crying about her parents' divorce. Better for killing a conversation than starting one.

Instead, me and Vern and Alfred claimed some chairs poolside and tried to look cool, laughing about things on our phones or talking about songs we liked or if our families had been to the beach yet this summer. Alfred's glasses kept slipping down his nose, and Vern peeled off his white t-shirt, uncovering his already sunburnt shoulders. His mom lobbed a tube of sunscreen his way, which he caught and set aside, rolling his eyes at us as if saving his skin would make him less of a man. Whenever we glanced over at Juliet, and she glanced back, we nodded, because even lifting a hand to wave seemed geeky or desperate.

The slats of the chairs had already waffled the backs of our legs by the time Mr. Wilkinson went over to Juliet and said something to her, pointed at us. When she got up and wandered over after that, we all seemed to forget our hands were attached to our arms. They hung stupid at our sides or drummed the armrests of the chairs or slugged the guy sitting next to us for no reason.

"Thought you came to swim," she said. Her voice was halfway mocking, halfway almost shy. I stammered a shred of something about art class, but only a few broken syllables bumbled out, and she didn't even hear those. "You should get in. I'll be back in a minute. I just have to change." The open collar of her oversized shirt tilted to one side, and she pulled it straight again before walking off.

Vern said, "Y'all thinking what I'm thinking?" which was how he introduced every one of his ideas. He never waited for an answer, so there was no telling if any of us ever thought what he thought, but we all did what he said. "Let's go see what we can see." He bounced his eyebrows toward the house, meaning we should go spy on Juliet changing her clothes. "The whole fucking house is made of glass," he said. "It's built for it."

"She wouldn't have told us what she was doing if she hadn't expected us to follow her," Alfred said. He pushed his glasses up his nose and breathed in loud through his mouth. "Would she?"

"Yeah, and even the way she's walking," Vern said. "You can tell she knows we're watching."

The front of the house faced the pool, and the back faced Afton Mountain and the National Forest that clung to it like hair. No neighbors for miles in that direction. Driving up, you couldn't miss the sun glinting off all that glass. You couldn't help but know the whole thing was see-through.

Juliet followed the rest of the pebbly driveway from the pool toward her house. A thin strand of woods, maybe fifty yards deep, stood on both sides of it. With every swing of Juliet's hips, Vern puffed little noises.

"As soon as she's out of sight, we'll sneak up there," he said. "We don't want anybody to think we followed her." He always had a plan. "We'll go through the woods, like we're just goofing around."

Sweat and spider webs clung to our skin, and twigs and fallen sycamore gumballs pricked our feet. Vern cranked fart noises from his armpit like he'd been doing since third grade. His laugh still shrieked and cracked, same as before his voice changed. He didn't notice he was the only one laughing.

Alfred shushed him. "What if she hears?"

At the tree line, I hung back, and Alfred hovered beside me until Vern clapped him on the shoulder, shoving him forward. The force of the blow knocked his glasses lower on his nose again.

"It's go time," Vern said. "At the house, we'll each take a corner, and if you see something, say something. I bet we'll see everything. It'll be sweet." The same word he used right before playing this porn clip he'd favorited on his phone. He replayed that clip in the locker room after gym class, at his kitchen table when we did homework and his mother wasn't home, and even in the morning at the bus stop in our neighborhood. Sometimes girls would walk up, like Kelly Jackson, start to say hi, catch sight of the movie going in Vern's hand, then drain pale and back away at his freakish laugh.

Momentum, even some kind of wacked out logic, carried us through the woods and lasted up until we fanned out, alone. Each of us had an equal chance of finding the window where Juliet was changing. Or of not seeing anything. Maybe she would change in a bathroom or close her curtains, or maybe her bedroom was on the top floor, too high for us to see from the ground.

On my own, from the spot Vern chose for me, I had a hard time making myself look toward the glass. When I tried, I glimpsed a purple bedspread. A poster of a cat on a wall. A dresser with its drawers half opened and clothes hanging off the sides. Around one corner Vern was cursing his great view of the kitchen and, in the other direction, Alfred was kneeling on the ground feeling around for his glasses.

It was almost as hard to look away as it was to look, so I did both, until there was Juliet, her back to the window. She plucked at her shirt again, adjusting it, even though she was alone and even though she was about to take it off. Something lonesome about the gesture made my stomach swish. This wasn't just some girl on a porn clip on Vern's greasy phone.

In the kiln closet that one time, we were collecting our ceramic projects. Mine was a sad-looking dragon. The tongue fell off in the kiln and the glaze I'd used faded to a pale snotty green. Hers was a little vase with flower shapes glazed onto the sides, but she dropped it, and it smashed. She made a fast choking sound and started to cry before she remembered I was standing there. Tears waited in her eyes, and she held her breath and fluttered her hand in front of her face, waving to stop them from falling.

"It'll be okay," I said, "I'll help," and I knelt and gathered the pieces from the floor.

"No, no," she said. "That's not why I'm crying." I spilled the pieces into her open hands. "My parents just split. My mom moved out last night." She looked at me then, her eyes tense with hurt and confusion. Then she closed her eyes and let the tears fall.

I didn't know what to say. She was pretty and perfect, and I was gangly and nervous. "I'm sorry," was the best I could come up with.

She nodded, a sort of thank you, and held her breath again, trying to force herself back into control, and I took my dragon and left her there. When she came out again and sat back down with her friends, I had the feeling none of them knew what she'd told me.

Vern made it sound like spying on her was supposed to be so hot, but it felt gross. And now, she was standing there in the window, seeing me. Caught, the blood washed out of me, left me feeling shrunken and embarrassed. I wanted to be away from there. To never have been there.

I put both hands up in front of me, like the motion might convince her there was some other reason for me to be standing there, any other reason than why I was. She skewered me with her eyes, like a fork through a chicken leg, and jammed both her middle fingers in my direction. Her face looked angry, but also as hurt and undefended as that day in the closet. Then, the sun burst from behind a drift of fast-moving clouds and ricocheted off the side of the house, lighting the whole thing up like a sheet of orange fire, and I couldn't see her anymore.

Alfred circled around the house from his corner. "Hey, man, anything over here?" he whispered. I didn't answer, just made a break for the woods.

I ran until I stubbed my toe into a tree stump and jammed it. The scrape bled. I slumped down onto the stump and curled my head into my hands. I wanted to wait there until it was time to go home, but I knew I had to get back to the pool and act like nothing happened or else my dad would come looking for me and yell at me for ditching the boss's party.

The stone wall closest to the grill end of the pool was only ten or so yards from where I sat, and a heavy scent of barbecue drifted toward me. Vines heaped onto the wall, making it even taller than it was, so I couldn't see the people on the other side and they couldn't see me. But I could hear them, along with the not-so-distant sizzle of cooking meat.

It was a bunch of the dads. Even Mr. Wilkinson. They were laughing about something. I could hear a faint trickle of music, a tune that sounded familiar. It started slow and sped up, then the dads all laughed louder.

"What is this?" one of them asked.

"It's my son's phone." Vern's dad. "Can you believe this shit?" The music played again. It was the porn clip. The dads roared.

"Used to be all magazines," another one of the dads said.

"Kids these days with all their technology." My dad.

"You think I should say anything to him about it?" Vern's dad.

"What would you say? Boys will be boys."

"Quick, put it back. Before the wives see."

First they played the clip one more time. Their laughter sliced the air, high pitched, hysterical.

The woods livened up behind me, and Vern and Alfred scuffed into view. "Yo, man, what happened to you?" Vern asked.

I knew he meant why had I bolted, but I showed them my toe. It had started to purple and there was blood and torn flesh.

"Shit," Alfred said.

"Well, you didn't miss anything," Vern said. "That was a fucking waste of time. All of a sudden she popped out the front door in her suit with a towel around her waist."

I stood up and we started walking together again. I tried not to limp.

"Didn't see jack shit," Alfred said, hiking his glasses back up his nose. "But at least she didn't see us."

Back on the slates, we shucked off our shirts and stashed them at our seats. Vern's phone was back with his shoes, and Juliet was back at her lounge chair, lying flat with sunglasses hiding her eyes. Maybe she wouldn't say anything about seeing me. Walking by her, I looked the other way and clenched and unclenched my fingers, wishing I was invisible.

We shove-splashed each other into the ten feet and took turns trying out flips on the diving board. Eventually the water stopped stinging the gash on my toe. Every now and then, Juliet would look over at us. All the air sucked out of me when she stood up and joined the line to dive.

"Hey, boys," she said. Her lips hung in a smirk and her eyes zeroed in on me. "Get your eyeful?"

Vern snorted and slammed me in the shoulder. "Nice, man. No wonder you ran off." Nearby, the grill smoked and barbecue fumes started to make me feel sick.

"You do that kind of thing a lot? Sneak peeks into people's windows?" Juliet said. She didn't shout, but she wasn't quiet either.

Mr. Wilkinson separated from the other dads, then sized us up, one at a time. A leg of chicken caught fire on the grill. The smell of the burning sauce mixed with fresh cut grass, chlorine, and the smell of last year's leaves on the forest floor—a perfect summer smell. Mr. Wilkinson stepped over there without losing eye contact with us and flipped the chicken leg, dousing the flame that way, giving him an extra second to think.

"What'd you boys do?" he asked. Mrs. Wilkinson shifted her sunglasses up into her hair to get a better view. Little wavelets in the pool sparkled with sunshine like a thousand tiny stars floating there.

Juliet stared me down and I was sure she was waiting for me to confess. Even if I'd wanted to, I wouldn't have been able to find my voice. But she answered for us anyway. "What'd you expect them to do, Daddy?"

Little kids kept splashing in the shallow end, but at the deep end everything stopped. No one jumped off the diving board. The moms swiveled to face us. The dads put down their beers.

"I mean, everything here, this huge house, the fancy pool, every tiny driveway stone," Juliet said. "It's all for people to look at, right?" Her eyes forked her father into place instead of me now. "That's why you invited these nice men from work, isn't it? To look at all your fancy things? Your great big house? Your new beautiful wife? Such an upgrade from boring old Mom." Our moms shifted in their chairs and straightened bathing suit straps, fluffed their hair.

"Juliet," came her father's voice, warning. Her stepmother's half smile curled to one side like a question mark.

A beach ball smacked the water at the edge of the pool beside Alfred. A couple of preschoolers in the shallow end clapped their hands for him to throw it back. But no one did.

"It's all about showing off, isn't it? I can show off too." And she reached back to the nape of her neck, pinched the knot of her bikini top between two fingers, and made like she was untying it. I didn't believe what Vern had said anymore, that she might want to be looked at that way, but Vern and Alfred jerked to attention while Mr. Wilkinson lunged to stop her.

The barbecue tongs clattered to the slates, and a spray of sauce splattered Juliet's chest before her father charged into her, knocking her backwards into the pool, his own body crashing in after hers. Their two splashes merged and thrashed a wave of water into our shins where we still stood, no longer waiting for the diving board.

Juliet rose to the surface, choking with laughter. Her bikini top had come untied for real when she dunked into the water—you could see how the straps had gone loose—but she managed to keep hold of them behind her neck. In front of me, Vern let out a quiet hissing whistle under his tongue.

"Shut up, asshole," I said.

He faced me, stunned. "What the hell?"

"Language, boys," one of the mothers called.

"Leave her the fuck alone," I said.

With her top re-tied and perfect again, Juliet doggy paddled toward the ladder near us. "My hero," she sneered.

The rest of the parents turned quickly back to their conversations and beverages, looking away as Mr. Wilkinson heaved himself out of the pool, his pink polo and madras shorts coursing with water. His eyes, little stones of hatred, fastened on me, but what could he say to me now?

Vern shoved my shoulder and walked past me and away, leaving me alone at the deep end. At the grill, the chicken legs burned to char, filling the air with rotten sweetness.

Next to the Fortune-Teller's House

We lived here six months before the sign went up—a red neon hand, as tall as me standing. Before the sign, we didn't know what all those people wanted with her, our gray-haired neighbor in her boho clothes. Now people queue up to wait for the neon palm to click on in the morning. Used to be, they lined up with the light of day.

It's too early now for lines. A distant, smoky scent woke me, and I hobble, half-blind, to the window that looks out toward the fortune-teller's property. Fifty yards or so downhill from her house, a hundred yards from mine, a smudge of light smolders.

Our houses front the back road to the airport. Our yards are long and wide. Beyond us on one side, For Sale signs pepper undeveloped woods and predict strip malls and office parks. On the other side, immediately beyond the fortune-teller's house, stands a gas station. We're all either of us has for neighbors.

A few times before the sign, I brewed a pot of tea, arranged ginger cookies on a plate, and gathered it all onto a tray. Once, I made it halfway across my yard before cars started pulling up in the fortune-teller's driveway. I'd seen them before, but the steady streams always surprise. Some are priests, others cops. What do they ask? What can she tell them?

She can't be awake over there yet. No light shines from the house, though the front yard flames grow brighter as I watch. My husband grunts from the sheets, half asleep, "Evelyn? Are you coming back to bed?"

If I'd made it over to the fortune-teller's house that first time with the cookies and the tea, I would have asked her, What will my baby be when she grows up? Will she look more like my husband or me? Will she be happy? But shortly after my first attempt at a visit, that baby died inside me.

The next time I was ready to spread more cookies and tea on a tray, I would've asked simpler things—Will this baby have all its toes? Curly hair or straight?

After the second one died, I was afraid to meet the fortune-teller at all. Afraid to learn if I'd get pregnant again or if another baby might die. Even if I chose not to ask her anything, I was afraid of what I'd see in her eyes when we met. I started to dislike her.

I move to the front of the house to another window that frames the fortune-teller's yard. The little fire wavers into the darkness. Is it part of a ritual? I don't think so, but I don't know what sorts of things fortune-tellers might go in for.

I do know she's a gardener. Rare moments when there are no lines of people waiting, she crouches in her yard, tending her plants. Butterflies light on her hair. Her garden is perfect with blossoms. She positions cement benches in thoughtful spaces under trellises and tall shrubbery. Sometimes, the people waiting for her sit there, seeming to be calmed by the living things around them.

For every baby who dies, I plant a lilac or rose of Sharon in our yard. Every spring of every year we live here their blossoms will remind me of the babies whose lives slipped away before I could touch their warm, petal-smooth skin.

I'm afraid I'll have a fat healthy hedge as an old, old lady, and no children, no grandchildren. Just beautiful shrubs and tiny, fey ghosts swirling through the greenery.

Smoke thickens across the way. Could the clouds buffeting toward my yard carry some kind of signal with them?

At the fortune-teller's house lately, a man visits whenever the sign is off. I can't see him clearly from our yard, but he's burly with a rough-sounding voice that I can hear whenever the wind aims it our way. He has shouted at her once or twice, a sound like bricks clapping together. I'm not the fortune-teller, but there's something wrong about that man.

As much as a year has passed since I last thought of going next door to meet my neighbor, a year since I became afraid of her. Now is my fourth pregnancy.

I wake up each morning thinking of polar bears. When it isn't cold enough for them anymore, they will die. One day, there will be a last one. Is today my baby's last day? My body her shrinking ice cap?

If you say something like that with a doctor listening, something mystical and worried, they prescribe pregnancy-friendly antidepressants or refer you to a support group. I don't want these things. All I want is my babies.

The fire eats away at a bush in one of the many landscaped areas of the fortune-teller's yard, near one of her benches. I can picture that man who visits her, sneaking from their bed under the cover of darkness, dousing her favorite bush with gasoline, tossing a match. Did she know at the first soft look in that man's eye that he would turn into a devil and bring destruction? And did she choose to love him anyway, for as long as his gentleness lasted?

Behind me my nightgown trails the high, late-spring meadow grass that separates our houses. The burning bush crackles in my ears. I rush past the bonfire heat of it, then cut toward the house, short of breath. My feet scratch against dry grass and tiny rocks.

At the fortune-teller's door, I drape one hand across my belly. Maybe my lost babies have known the feeling of my arm's cradle, at least. The first hint of dawn grays the sky. I pound the door in the shadow of the tall palm-shaped sign, now dark. A few cars curl away on the road in front of our houses.

What will I do if that burly man is still here? If he answers the door?

Somehow I know the fire is all he left behind.

I've never seen the fortune-teller up close. Her face pinches with wrinkles, like a wizened fruit left on a windowsill. She looks weary. She doesn't stand straight, leans into the door when she opens it. My hand reaches toward hers. "I saw the fire. Are you all right?"

"Fire?" she says, not alarmed exactly. She wasn't awake before my knock. She casts a glance over my shoulder, sees the flames from the bush licking the sky above it. She nods. "Fire." A look of resignation overtakes the features of her face. She opens the door wider for me.

I step inside. "I'm so sorry."

She nods again and leads me to her kitchen. Her white nightgown is thin as paper, and her feet are bare. Her hands dangle, empty, at her sides. Like a little child. I think how everyone is a little child.

"Let's have some tea," she says, and she can tell I've figured out something very sad and secret about her life. This is a morning like dozens of other mornings she's had already and like dozens yet to come. I'm sorry to know this.

When she pours the tea, she sits across from me at her breakfast table. Her feet don't touch the ground. "I'm

Evelyn," I say. "I've meant to come meet you, ever since we moved in."

"I know," she says, but she doesn't mean it in a fortune-telling way. "It isn't easy to visit me with all the people coming and going. I've meant to come meet you too, but then the next one comes." She waves her hand toward the front door. I picture fortunes, like liquid, draining from her over the years. She must be very tired.

"Should we put out the fire?" I say.

"No, it'll be all right, Evelyn."

I don't know if this is a fortune or not, if she means the fire will put itself out or that the man will not come back, or if she means this baby will live. It doesn't matter. This is just a cup of tea with the fortune-teller next door, who is soon to be my friend, and everything will be all right.

Sorry Enough

Now, when Buckley sees people he knows in places like the Food Lion, they take a minute to recognize him. Since the accident, Buckley has grown a beard, and the prison-issue buzz cut has replaced his shaggy-dog hair. His year inside cost him a good fifteen pounds too, taking him from his usual lean all the way to lanky. People not knowing him at first is what gave Buckley the idea to knock on Ida Nevins's door. Ida is the woman he hit with his car—hit and run. The one he went to prison for.

Ida's is a squat white stucco house with a green front door and matching shutters in the Charlottesville neighborhood jammed up behind the Salvation Army. The houses cramp together there in tight crooked rows like multi-colored teeth. In the two weeks Buckley's been out, he's gone out of his way to walk by Ida's house five or six times. He's noticed that her yard is pretty and lush at the end of a rainy summer. The crape myrtles are at the end of their bloom, their petals making bright pink confetti on the ground. Sunflowers wave on heavy heads alongside her shed.

Still, Buckley can see where she could use some help. The yard extends beyond the shed, and back there the weeds stand knee high. The shrubs out front are due for a trim. The shed could use a fresh coat of paint.

Each time he's walked by Ida's house, he's been the only white guy around, and today is no different. Men loitering at the bottom of the street turn in Buckley's direction, giving him the stink eye as he steps onto the sidewalk leading to Ida's front porch. Buckley got used to being an odd white face in a crowd when he was in jail, where he met plenty of guys serving longer sentences for far less than he'd done.

He notices paint peeling on the black metal railing up the steps of Ida's porch—one more job that needs doing. Pots of bright red begonias flank the front door. He knocks.

Besides growing a beard and losing enough weight to change the whole shape of his face, another thing Buckley did in jail was get sober. Before jail, he'd led what his last girlfriend, Scarlett had called a slacker life—painting houses by day with his friend Tuck's business, playing bass guitar with The Electric Chinchillas by night. In a life like that, one day bled into the next, and every bleary, drunken night felt the same.

Now that he's out, Buckley wants everything about his life to be different, better. His first step is to find a way to do something good for Ida. He can't undo what he did, can't un-slam her body from against his car, can't un-damage her. But he can do some hard work on her behalf. If she'll let him.

His bristle-short hair and patchy, new-growth beard make him feel somehow top-heavy, and Buckley suspects that his chin juts forward on his neck when he stands. So he tries to tuck in his rib cage and pull in his chin while he waits at the door. He's about to knock a second time when he hears clacking and shuffling from inside. Slippers on hard wood? A cane?

"Yes?" comes a woman's voice. Through the sliver opening of the door, Buckley can see the pink piping on the wrist of Ida's housecoat, and, beyond Ida, only darkness. A shaft of sunlight makes a starburst on her glasses and shines off the thick gold chain that extends from the earpieces and disappears behind her neck. The top of Ida's mostly silvered head comes to Buckley's chest. He doesn't remember her being so small.

"Ma'am," Buckley says, looking down at her. "My name is Philip." He wants to make something better for her, but he doesn't want her to know he's the one doing it. Lucky for him, the only photos Ida could have seen of him were the lousy mug shots the paper ran all those weeks when the story was new. So he re-straightens his posture, tweaks his new-growth beard. "I noticed some things around your yard might need tending to."

"Not interested," Ida says, her voice gravel rough.

Buckley flattens his palms in a gesture to keep her from shutting the door all the way. "Please, ma'am," he says. Walking by here so many times, he had come up with a few ideas for how to sell his plan to her. "It's for a service project."

"I don't care for any charity."

Buckley inches closer, still extending his flattened palms toward the closing door. "No ma'am, please. I've gone about this the wrong way. What I need is, I fell on some hard times recently, and I'm trying to re-establish myself." The shreds of truth to this excuse make the words come easily. "If you could help me out here, I'd like to offer my services in exchange for a letter of recommendation, something to help me get more business later on."

Ida lets the door swing open a little more, though she holds one hand fast to the doorknob. She keeps her lips screwed tight, giving off the feeling that she's still waiting for him to try to sell her something she doesn't want. With the door open wider, Buckley can see the back of a faded brown recliner, a white lace doily draped at the head, a table of glass figurines catching the light from the window, walls painted pale blue.

He ad libs through a list of free services he hopes to provide—painting her shed and railings, mowing her lawn and weeding flower beds, cleaning out gutters and repairing her roof—always coming back to the huge favor she'll be doing him if she says yes. "I've got another job too," he says, hoping to boost his credibility, "so I'll have to schedule my work around that." He's careful not to elaborate. He has not one, but two other jobs. The first is a paid apprenticeship his parole officer set up for him, three days a week, at a local cabinet maker's shop. The second is as a late-shift convenience store clerk at Snappy's, down the hill from the house he's renting now. Buckley supposes both jobs sound about as pathetic as knocking on strangers' doors to ask them to let you work for them for free. "I'll be here, ma'am, with your permission, Tuesdays and Thursdays, until everything's all shaped up."

"All shaped up," Ida repeats, nodding. Finished listening, she steps backward into the darkness of her house.

"And thank you," Buckley says. "Thank you for giving me a chance." He finally lets her close the door.

———

Buckley arrives at Ida's yard the next Tuesday, nine a.m. sharp, hauling some tools in a borrowed trailer. Ida's sitting on a bench in her garden, a tortoiseshell-handled cane leaning next to her knee and a woman about her age, mid-sixties maybe, sitting beside her.

"Morning, ma'am," Buckley says to Ida.

She props one foot on a rock in front of her. The other woman stops mid-sentence to stare up at Buckley.

"I aim to start with the weeds behind your shed, if that's all right."

"That'll be just fine."

Buckley goes back to get the mower. He'd borrowed the trailer from Tuck, who won't hire him back as a painter—*Folks like to make sure no ex-cons go crawling around their houses, man. I have to promise them. Nothing personal*—but he's happy to loan Buckley equipment. The lawnmower is borrowed too, from the shed behind his house. The only way he can afford rent is to barter some handyman services around the place. The ragged old Pontiac the trailer's hooked to belongs to Buckley, though. It came cheap from his AA sponsor, Henry. The car that hit Ida sold at police auction after the trial, while Buckley was in jail. His new, special license only allows him to drive to and from work. He hopes this work counts.

To get to the weeds behind the shed, Buckley has to roll the mower past where the two women sit talking. He looks at Ida's cane, resting against the bench, and figures it must have been the accident that ruined her leg. He remembers some things about her from what he had read in the paper—she had been a guidance counselor at Jackson-Via Elementary, her husband is dead—but the papers never gave much detail about her injuries.

The women's heads swivel toward him as he approaches. Ida's friend says to her, "How'd you get a white boy doing your yard? Only white boys I ever see are up at the University dining hall. Complain about every last flavor. Leave more trash than they start out with. Never seen one of them lift a hand that didn't wind up doing their own selves a favor. White boy doing your yard." Her laugh rasps like sandpaper on metal.

Buckley figures they know he must be able to hear them, wonders if they mean to let him in on their joke. He keeps pushing the mower past them, but then Ida's friend calls out. "Scuse me." Her fuzzy white hair glints in the morning sun. "I got just one question for you, young man."

"Yes, ma'am?" Already the sun is hot. He drags a bandana across his forehead, then re-stashes it in his back pocket.

"Why Ida's yard?" She gestures around them, indicating the sweep of houses, the street, the men smoking cigarettes down by the stop sign.

Buckley stares until his eyes dry out—which happens fast because he can't think of an explanation. "As good a place as any."

Ida's friend likes his answer, winks at him. "You come find my yard next, y'hear? It's good a place as any too. Even better. Better place as any."

It's hot. The sun hits hard behind the shed. Buckley trades between weeding the sunflower bed and mowing the tall weeds, clearing the blades every few minutes to keep the mower from choking to death.

The yard is bigger than it seemed from the sidewalk. It stretches long and narrow behind Ida's house. Buckley figures it could total half an acre, with big rocks to mow around and a few steep slopes that require every muscle in his arms.

In jail, Buckley had always volunteered for the work crews, anything to get outside. He didn't care how cars passing by would know the instant they saw his orange jumpsuit that he was doing time, didn't care that no one ever looked closer to see if they knew him, assuming every guy in prison must be a stranger, even though, there he was—Buckley Sanford, Ted and Judy's boy.

People knew the Sanfords. His parents owned gas stations around town, hobnobbed at fund-raising galas. Every year his mom or dad won some new civic award. Buckley's accident had made headlines for weeks. Everyone who'd heard of him or his family knew all about it. Picking up trash with the other inmates on the road crew, Buckley watched plenty of people he knew drive past, their windows sealed tight against the cold or the heat or the rain, while he stood knee-deep in ditches with soggy diapers and used condoms in his hands.

He didn't mind. Hard work released him, hushed the continual audio replay of Ida's body thumping into his bumper, then up onto the hood. The sound her head made.

Buckley's glad the mower is loud, that it shivers so much in his grip that his hands have gone numb. He's glad he's so hot that sweat pours off him. He peels away his t-shirt, tucks it into the waistband of his jeans and lets the sun burn the white, white skin of his back.

Mowing a last strip of yard, behind the house on an uphill slope to the neighbor's fence, he's surprised when he hears a voice close to his ears. He cuts the mower engine, and there's Ida.

"It's time for a break." She holds a small turquoise plate with a neatly halved sandwich, a mound of potato chips, grapes. Using one hand to grip her cane, the other to carry the sandwich, Ida limps, leading Buckley toward the bench where she had sat earlier with her friend.

Judging by the sun and the scarcity of shade, Buckley guesses it's about noon. A tall glass of iced tea perches on the bench, slick with condensation. The promise of coldness makes his mouth water. "Thank you," he says, while shame flushes his face. This is the woman who rolled across his car, so hard she dented the hood.

The way Ida stands there, leaning into her cane, it looks like she means to stay awhile, to look after him while he eats. Last time anyone had looked after him was way before jail, lifetimes even.

"Your friend's gone?" Buckley asks.

"Mm-hmm. Mrs. Henshaw's from two streets over. We've been friends a thousand years, seems like."

Ham and cheese never tasted so good. Buckley tries to remember how long it's been since he's sat outside to eat on a pretty day. It would've been with Scarlett, maybe only a few weeks before the accident. He would've packed a six of beer, then drunk them all before they even got to the park. He can picture Scarlett's lips, seamed with disapproval. He's called her several times since he's been out, one of the few people from before that he's allowed himself to contact. She lets it ring.

Buckley worries that the sweat and heat might make him look more like he used to. "The sandwich was delicious," he says. He licks mustard from his fingertips. "But I better get back to work."

Ida collects his now-empty plate and glass, pinching them together in one hand to leave the other free for her cane. It must have taken her two trips when the glass was full.

———

Buckley's sponsor, Henry, stops in at Snappy's to check up on him. Henry lost an eye the last time he got drunk, hardly remembers doing it, just woke up half-blind in an alley the next morning. He's a short, squat, bald man with an eye patch, doing his best, one day at a time.

Buckley tells him how strange it feels to have so many things going right. Doug, at the cabinet shop, trains Buckley on a new tool or technique just about every week, says he has natural aptitude. Ida brings him lunches and compliments his progress in her yard. At the convenience store,

Buckely's always on time and his register rings out balanced after every shift.

Hot dog wieners rotate in a case behind him. He wipes coagulated grime from the mustard spout and explains to Henry how, before jail, people soured on him quickly, how he had painted with Tuck for three and a half years, but he knew his friend had only given him the easiest jobs. Paid him the least, "forgot" to tell him some days when a new job was starting up. Even with Scarlett, he could tell she had stopped thinking long-term after only a couple of months. It was easier for her to leave, then, when she stopped having fun. "I keep waiting to fuck up all over again."

"You can't keep fucking up just because you know how," Henry says. "It's a tightrope, man. You got to balance yourself believing you won't fall, then just try harder if you start to wobble."

Once upon a time, Henry had been a day trader with a wife and a house and a BMW. Now he's assistant manager at the Lowe's out at Zion Crossroads. "And I'm a happy man!" he declares, whenever he tells his own story, leaning both elbows into the podium at a meeting. "I could be fucking dead right now. Hell, I *should* be dead. Makes a job at Lowe's like a party every day, man. Every single fucking day."

"You think if I keep it up, all the good impressions, Scarlett'll come around?" Buckley says.

Henry rolls a pack of lifesavers between his palms. He always buys something when he visits Buckley at work. "Don't tell me you're getting clean for a girl, Buckley. You're smarter than that, man." For the past few weeks, Henry has been trying to convince Buckley to stop calling her, and everybody in the program, not just Henry, says, "The only person you can get clean for is yourself. Everything else backfires."

"Scarlett's not what you need to worry about, man," Henry says, before he claps Buckley's shoulder and reminds him, yet again, to call if he needs anything.

———————

One late September afternoon, Buckley's out mowing his own little strip of a yard, aproned around the tiny old house he rents on the corner of Chesapeake and Steephill Streets. Over the mower, he hears something, and, when he turns, he sees a car has pulled to the curb where his yard and Chesapeake meet.

He idles the mower and heads over toward the car. It's Ida, rolling down her window. "Well, well, well, Philip," she says. "Look at you, with other jobs already."

Buckley's heartbeat ratchets up in his chest. Here at home, any minute someone could come by and call him by his real name. Except that Buckley has avoided his old friends since he's been out and hasn't really made new ones, other than Henry. Even the old lady next door, whose garbage can Buckley always trundles back behind her house on trash days, doesn't know his name.

"This is my place, actually," Buckley says. The small house sits on a red-painted cinderblock foundation, nothing more than four rooms and some closets. He hardly has belongings to fill it with, so, even though it's small, inside has an empty feeling. After Buckley had gone to jail, his parents hired a company to clean out his old apartment. All they had saved of his things had fit into two paper grocery bags.

"You do a nice job in your own yard too," Ida says with an appraising nod.

"Thank you, ma'am." His throat tightens at the praise.

"I didn't know you lived around here." Ida looks up and down the street, maybe filing this spot into her memory, as if she might want to drop by someday on purpose. Buckley glances up and down the street too, checking again for anyone who might know him.

"Listen, Philip, I've been meaning to talk to you for a while now," Ida says. "You've done an awful lot of work for me. I can hardly justify letting you keep on. I'm ready to write any sort of letter for you to help you get some regular paying jobs."

"That's very kind of you, ma'am," Buckley says. "But I haven't finished painting your shed. I can't walk away from a job half done."

"A job half-done?" she says. "That's what you call all the work you've done? You're one hard worker, Philip."

―――――――

Buckley has lost track of how many times he's tried to call Scarlett when one night, not long before his shift at the convenience store, she answers. "You've got to quit calling me, Buckley."

Scarlett is a dancer with a finely sculpted body and hair as glossy as a baby doll's. He pictures her leaning against the wall at her place, the way she does sometimes when she's on the phone, hair falling around her face, free arm trailing down. Maybe she's wearing one of her flowing, sleeveless tops, some tight dance pants that hug her curves. It's weird after so long to have Scarlett's voice close and real in his ears—talking to him, scolding him, as if they had just spoken days before.

"I know I've been calling too much," Buckley says. "I just wanted to apologize to you, try to make amends."

"So you're sober now? Working your program?"

"Yes, actually, I am. I'm all about going forwards, not backwards."

"That'd make a great t-shirt," Scarlett says with a snort.

Hearing her voice and the rejection in it makes it hard for Buckley to swallow his pride rather than hang up, but he does his best, clamping the phone tighter, clearing his throat. "I owe you a lot of apologies," he says, "and I want you to know, I've been different since I got out. I don't hang out with any of the old guys or go to any of the old places." There are entire streets he avoids, miles and miles of them, where the bars he used to go to were, where his old friends had lived, places he had wandered drunk and stupid or pissed in alleys, puked in trash cans. The street where he hit Ida.

"Congratulations." Her voice is flat.

"Everything you ever said about me was true. I should've gotten a better job, cleaned myself up, paid better attention to you. I'm ashamed of myself. Drinking my way out of your life was the stupidest thing I've ever done."

"The stupidest thing, Buckley? Really?"

The noises he hates rush back in, the way they did every night in jail. All the other sounds in the cell block echoed. Not these—body thuds, dull moans. After Ida had scudded across his car, she landed stomach-down in the gutter, groaning. It was just past twilight in early May, dark enough that passing cars didn't notice what had happened right away.

Buckley had rushed out of his car, his head muzzy with drink, legs wobbling with adrenaline, and he crouched beside her in the growing darkness, mumbling, "God, oh God," while Ida kept up a low wail. He knew better than to move her—something he had picked up from cop shows on TV—but he didn't like how the side of her face pressed against pavement. He managed to fold his jacket and squeeze it gently under her cheek. Then he noticed her purse spilled in the road just beyond his car. First he grabbed for her cell phone and called for help, struggling against his drunkenness for words that made sense. "It's a woman. I hit a woman. With my car," and he gave the location. Then he gathered her things back into her purse, leaned it next to her. The way he had veered his car after Ida had fallen to the ground, it now protected her from oncoming traffic. As soon as the sirens were getting close and the first cars were beginning to pull over to see what was going on, Buckley took off running.

He had run because he was scared. Because if they caught him while he was still drunk it would count as his third DUI, and he'd lose his license. Because there had been nothing else he could do.

His jacket, under Ida's head, was where he kept his wallet with all his money and his ID, plus, of course, his car was registered in his name. Much later that night, when he finally made it home, police were waiting for him—one at the door, one in the cruiser parked out front.

"I'm sorry for that too," Buckley says, as if Scarlett could have known what had just replayed in his mind. When she makes a sound as if she means to get off the phone, he tries to stall her. "I think she likes me, though."

"What do you mean, she likes you, Buckley? How can she like you?" Now she sounds almost panicked.

"No, no, it's not what you think," he says, rushing his words. "She doesn't know it's me. I'm doing some work around her yard. For free."

"Buckley, that's crazy."

"It's not crazy," Buckley says. "I knew it wouldn't be right to just go up to her and apologize, like I had a right to do that or something. But I thought maybe if I did a bunch of stuff for her, I could be sorry that way."

"Shit, Buckley, you could never be sorry enough."

Buckley is October's employee-of-the-month at Snappy's. A green, grainy ink-jet version of his face is taped to the wall beside the lottery ticket display at the checkout counter. A couple days ago when his manager had told him he'd been chosen, he'd been happy. His grin on the blurry image shows that. But now all he can think of is what Scarlett might say. *That's the best you can do? Employee of the month at fucking Snappy's?* Before he had talked to her today, he'd forgotten how she spoke to him sometimes. How she never expects much from him.

Buckley studies the greenish cast to his simpering smile in the picture on the wall, then takes in the gently humming display of rotating hot dogs, the rows of corn nuts and potato chips, the candy-colored cases of beer sitting so neat and square at the back of the store. *That's the best you can do?* It doesn't help that Snappy's stays empty for most of Buckley's late evening shift, giving him nothing to distract him.

It seems like it's the cases of beer that walk up the length of the store to him, but of course it's the other way around. Once he has a can in his hand again, it fits. What does it matter? What does anything matter?

The first beer is for Scarlett, for probably never loving him. The second is for his family, for never calling to see how he is now, for never visiting him in jail. The third one is for jail, because what the fuck. After that, he stops counting.

First thing Buckley notices when he's awake again is how bright the sunlight is. His eyelids aren't thick enough. The light feels like an axe to his eyes. And he's cold.

His world is all sound for the moment. A trash truck lurches past, sounding closer than it should. Water drips nearby. It's not a bathroom faucet, but maybe a hose? And is that dew? From grass underneath him, seeping through his khaki pants? He louvers his eyelids against the sun, pats his chest. He's still wearing his green and yellow Snappy's apron. He smells vaguely of hot dogs. His back leans against the side of a shed, and he's facing a familiar back door.

Some of the blur of the night before clears. Sour remnants of last night's beer linger in his mouth. He remembers the vague notion that he needed to get to Ida's on time this morning because it's Tuesday and because she thinks he's reliable. Because he means to be reliable.

Slouching here like this—wearing off a drunk, ragged and reeking—he looks more like his old self than he has for months. He doesn't want Ida to find him this way and figure out who he really is. But even if she sees him and still thinks he's Philip, she'll know him for *what* he really is. He leans forward urgently. He needs to leave. But the motion whirls the ocean of his belly, hammers his head.

He'd like to run away again, but he doesn't think he can get very far. He lifts himself to his knees, but before he can manage to get himself up to standing, something rushes toward him—a confusion of faces and arms and legs. The men he's used to seeing down by the stop sign, they must be the men surrounding him now.

"Fuck you doing?" one of them says, shoving Buckley's shoulders and knocking him back to the ground. "Huh? White boy? What the fuck you doing here?"

Buckley fumbles for words to explain, but when he tries to stand again, someone's foot knocks into him, sending him backward one more time. The slam of his back against the shed forces him to retch into the grass beside him.

"Holy fuck, man," the same guy says. All three men jump away from the mess and stench.

The creak of a screen door catches their attention, and the men turn toward Ida's house. She stands on her back stoop in the housecoat with the pink piping. "What's all this ruckus about, boys?"

The man who had shouted at Buckley is about a foot taller than the other two, his shoulders rounded as if to apologize for his height. He faces Ida now, subdued. "Sorry, Mrs. Nevins," he says. "We were keeping an eye out for you, ma'am. Saw this man in your yard, wanted to make sure he didn't mean you no harm."

Ida leans against the doorframe for a better view. Buckley looks down, trying to hide himself.

"Philip?" she says.

"You know this guy?" one of the shorter men says.

"He's the young man who's been working in my yard."

All the men do double-takes, make sounds of recognition. "What the fuck you doing, man?" the tall guy repeats, more puzzled than angry now.

"Watch your language, please, Charles," Ida says, in a tone that suggests she has known this man since he was a child. "Now can y'all help me get him into the kitchen? He looks mighty unsteady."

The two shorter men brace Buckley's body under his arms on either side. The tall man, Charles holds the door. They drag Buckley gently up the steps of Ida's back stoop and into her bright kitchen where they deposit him onto the black and white tile floor. He slumps against her cabinets. The refrigerator hums beside him, its face cluttered with photos of babies, children, and families. People Ida must know and love. What Buckley realizes is that this is what he's wanted for himself—to be a face on someone's refrigerator, with a magnet holding him tight and fast, proving that he matters somewhere.

Charles speaks again, quietly to Ida, making sure she'll be safe with Buckley. "He won't hurt me," she says.

After the men leave, Ida sets a pot of coffee to brew. She hasn't said anything to Buckley yet, hasn't looked him in the eye. An ill-flavored scrim of post-binge filth coats the inside of his mouth, and he fears that its foulness, his foulness will infect the entire room.

"Not your usual self this morning," Ida says, handing Buckley a damp rag to clean himself up with, then turning her back to him to putter with coffee mugs.

"I certainly hope not, ma'am."

When she delivers steaming coffee, he looks at the mug rather than her face. "Thanks, ma'am. I'll just have a few sips, clear my head, then I'll get myself out of your way."

"Suit yourself." Ida holds her own coffee cup in one hand, leans the other on her cane, and eases her way toward the kitchen table. She pulls out one of the bright yellow vinyl-covered chairs and sits. "Must've been some reason you hauled yourself over here in this state, though. Any idea what that was?"

"I have a railing to finish painting," he tells her. "I was thinking about that." He rubs a hand over his face, the bristle of his unshaven chin scratching his palm. "But I shouldn't have come. I don't want you to see me this way."

"Why's that?" Ida asks. "Why don't you want me to see you this way?" She holds her coffee cup in both her hands and looks squarely at him. "Just exactly how do you think I see you?"

He gestures at himself with one hand—as if with one motion he could indicate all his weaknesses, from the state of his grass-stained khakis, the stench of his breath, all the way into the core of his soul. "Not like this."

Ida chuckles. "You really think I don't know who you are, *Philip*?" She lets the fake name unroll slowly off her tongue. She taps her finger—*plink, plink*—against the rim of her coffee cup.

The room sloshes a little side to side, and Buckley, feeling every beat of his heart in his temples, looks up at Ida now, so anchored, prim, and straight.

"I knew you the second you walked up my front walk, Buckley Sanford," she says. "How could I not know? I saw you that night. You got out of the car that hit me, smelling exactly like you do now. I saw you then, and I saw you in the paper too. I looked you right in your eyes."

Buckley feels dizzy and a little afraid. "But why would you let me help you, then? Let me anywhere near you?"

"Aw, Buckley, listen to yourself. By the time you screwed up your nerve to knock on my front door, you'd long since finished any harm you'd ever do to me." Ida sets down her mug. "When you showed up here, I knew the only person you weren't finished harming was yourself."

Buckley sips the coffee, so hot it burns his tongue. "Is that supposed to make me feel better?"

"Lord, son, what on earth makes you think you're supposed to feel better?"

Now Buckley meets her eyes. "I didn't mean to hurt you," he says, feeling every bit as pathetic as he must look.

"I never thought you meant to," Ida says, her voice almost a whisper. "But that doesn't mean it won't take you a long time to feel better." She hobbles with her cane to the sink, beside Buckley, and dumps the last of her coffee, rinses the cup. "The pain I wake up with every day is just pain. I could name it Buckley, if I felt like it. I could wake up every morning and curse the day you were born. But what good would that do?" She rests her hand for a moment on Buckley's shoulder. "The pain you wake up with is another story. You came here thinking it had something to do with me. But look at me," Ida says, flicking one hand toward herself. "I'm just fine."

Ida stands beside him while he finishes his coffee, every hot sip making him feel a little more human. When the cup is empty, she takes it from him and rinses it, sets it beside her own in the sink.

"You go on and clean yourself up today, Buckley. And after that, you keep yourself clean, y'hear?" she says. Then she braces herself with one hand against the counter and reaches her other hand toward Buckley.

Her grip is strong. He lets her help pull him to standing, feels the wobble to his legs. "What if I can't?"

"You just decide you can," she says.

Outside, Buckley rubs his aching head in the too bright sun. He unties the Snappy's apron and balls it in his hands. Another lost chance. He'll hit a meeting before he even hits the showers.

The men at the stop sign nod in Buckley's direction as he walks away. Charles calls out, "Hey, man. Take it easy, a'ight?" They know exactly who he is now.

No Good

At the old house, Leslie had walked to school. Here, the school was closer, but she had to take the bus. The old house had been on the outskirts of a smaller town, not a former murder capital of the world. Leslie's mother had grown up only a few miles away from the new place and worried about drug crime crossfire and dirty old men. "It isn't safe," was her excuse for everything. "Trust me. I know."

What did she know, though? Treating the new neighborhood like a disease in need of a cure when it was Leslie's only antidote for summer boredom. With the divorce still fresh, her usual summer plans—sleepaway camps, swim and tennis teams, horseback riding day camps—had gotten lost in the confusion of who was to pay for what. Leslie didn't mind missing out on the camps. What she minded was the chronic sameness of the open-ended days and the beep-beep of her cell phone's alarm, five minutes ahead of curfew, always cutting her nights short.

They had moved right before Leslie finished eighth grade, so she'd had time to make a few friends before summer break. "Don't be late!" her mother shouted after her whenever Della from down the street came calling.

This summer, Leslie had grown out of everything: shoes, shorts, her first bras. Surely she'd grown into something too. Even an extra fifteen minutes would have seemed like recognition of that. "There's nothing but no good going

51

on out there after eleven," was the answer any time Leslie argued for more time, as if all the drug dealers and perverts poured onto the streets at the single stroke of a minute hand.

The only chance for excitement was Robby Newton, two years older and nearly a foot taller, who only seemed to come out after dark. Della and Leslie managed to track him down almost every night.

Tonight, they found him down by the basketball courts. First, they shot baskets with someone's lost tennis ball. Then they plunked quarters into the tennis court lights and chucked the ball back and forth across the sagging net before Robby beaned it into the woods behind them. Then they walked around the backyards of Lester Street to visit Mrs. Foster's kittens under her deck. Tonight, there were only four. Robby cupped one into his palm and flipped it over to show how its eyes were still closed, how its body clutched in toward itself like it hadn't finished uncurling from its momma's belly.

"Put it back," Della said. "You're not supposed to touch them."

"Who says?" Robby said.

"Who says you can?" Leslie watched the tone of Della's voice register on Robby's face, a tremor of skin under one eye. "Anyway," Della said, "I think it's something about smell. That kittens have to smell right to their mother?"

The kitten looked fragile in Robby's big hands, but if they annoyed him, he wouldn't hang out with them anymore. "I've never heard that," Leslie said, and she hadn't, but she felt queasy until he nestled the kitten back where it belonged.

The humid air clung to their skin as they rounded back toward the tennis courts. The timer for the lights ticked the last of their quarters' minutes away. Mosquitoes nattered at their ears and noses. Moths and gnats thronged at the lights, banging for their share of brightness.

A little after ten, Robby led them all into the woods behind the tennis courts. He and Leslie matched strides along the narrow path. The bristle of his arm hair against hers sent a thrill through her. The last of the evening's lightning bugs blinked on and off, flashing bright haloes of light into the thickening dark. Robby quickened his pace. Rushing after him, Leslie almost lost her footing on a rock.

"You can't even see the poison ivy this way," Della said somewhere behind them. Then a thump. "Shit. You can't see tree roots either."

Robby's arm brushed Leslie's again. She hadn't realized she'd caught up with him or that he was lurking so near her in the dark. Her body buzzed with the shape of his presence beside her.

"I'm going back," Della said.

"Oh don't go," Robby said, his voice flat and sarcastic. In the shadows beside Leslie, he leaned toward her and whispered, "Really, don't go. I want to show you something."

Della fumbled her way back up to her feet and brushed dirt from her shorts. The tennis court lights still winked through the trees in the distance, enough to guide her back out of the woods.

"You don't have to come with me," Della said.

Robby slipped his hand into Leslie's and rooted her in place. Della was Leslie's first friend here, and she knew she should go with her, but Robby's hand radiated heat all the way up her arm and down into her belly.

"Are you sure you can get home okay?" Leslie asked, and she let Della walk away alone. Then Robby pulled her toward the deeper woods. After a dogleg in the path, Leslie couldn't see the lights behind her anymore. She hoped they stayed lit long enough for Della to find her way out.

The only noises were bugs and frogs and, farther away, cars. Robby tugged, and they started running, twigs breaking underfoot, low-hanging branches scraping their arms and faces. Leslie didn't mind the scratches with Robby's hand pulsing in her own. This was what she'd been waiting for. She imagined getting to whatever spot he was dragging them to and what his body would feel like pressing against hers.

Her lips felt cracked and dry all of a sudden, and her tongue too thick in her mouth. What if she didn't know what to do when he kissed her? Where to put her tongue, her hands? She'd only had one other kiss, and that had been in fast motion under mistletoe in the back of her fifth-grade classroom, three years ago now. Like a warm little slug pushing in and out of her mouth. The rest of the class had already gone outside for recess. She'd left the room embarrassed, but with her heartbeat pounding in her ears. Running now made her heart beat louder and faster too, made her breath come short.

Robby jerked them to a stop at a cluster of vines and trees. Inside the thicket, fallen branches leaned toward each other making a twiggy tent. A string hung down from the opening, and a rag swayed from it in the middle of the air.

This was what he wanted to show her? A child's fort with a wilted flag?

A creek flowed with a noise like wind chimes beyond a row of scrubby bushes behind them. The moon had just begun to rise, huge and brilliant, and the waving rag flared white in its bright sudden light.

Robby made a low noise like a laugh. That was when Leslie recognized the rag for what it was. The missing kitten from Mrs. Foster's backyard. A breeze surged with the smell of wet earth from the creek and rocked the dead kitten back and forth.

She wanted to run, but Robby's hand clamped her in place. He sneered in the silver light, as if he were waiting for questions to dawn on her. Why would he do such a thing? Why would he show her? What would he do next?

Leslie's phone beeped twice. Robby jumped at the quick, shrill blasts. She took the chance to yank her hand from his.

"My mom'll kill me if I'm late." She shrugged like she was sorry, then ran like hell.

For a long time she couldn't see a thing around her. More twigs jabbed and scratched her. Uneven ground threatened to trip her. She was afraid to slow down in case Robby was right behind her. Even when she found her way to pavement, and then to a familiar street, she kept sprinting.

Nothing was enough to bring her home on time.

"Where were you?" her mother asked. She'd been waiting inside the door when Leslie clambered in. Standing there, her arms tied like a knot in front of her chest, her mother looked like a stranger. Hair frazzled, eyes hazy, always so tired here in their new life, with a job thirty minutes away she didn't like, new worries over paying bills, loud angry phone calls with Leslie's dad.

"What happened, Leslie? You're shaking." Her tone switched from scolding to alarmed.

Out of breath, Leslie slammed and locked the door behind her. She sank to the floor, staying clear of the windows in case anyone peeped in from outside.

"You're bleeding," her mother said and reached toward her face, crisscrossed with twig scratches. Outside in the damp heat, Leslie hadn't felt the blood, but the chill of the air conditioning made the ooze feel warm against her cooling flesh.

"Don't." Leslie swatted her mother's hand away.

She could feel the power of her mother's desire to help, the effort it took her to keep from reaching out to touch her again, but the world she had taught Leslie to fear didn't exist. The one that did was scarier. Leslie pressed her back tight against the door, as if she could be strong enough to keep it out by herself.

Heart Blown Through

DeMarco's reeks of nachos, onion rings, and decades of beer-soaked floorboards. A half dozen university students shoot darts in the back. A mop-headed guy at least half Irv's age nods at him from the bar. Irv tugs out a stool and orders a whiskey. Scoops a fist of pretzels from a bowl along the bar to mix with the salad souring in his belly and give the whiskey a place to land. How many people besides him walk into bars when they don't know what else to do? Must be a lot, but everybody else here seems like they mean to be.

One minute Mary was sitting on the edge of the bed, pulling up her socks for the morning. Next, she pitched over, twisting and dry coughing on the floor, one sock on, the other still in her hand. It was a heart attack, a faulty valve, they said. Now, she's been teetering in some twilight world of never waking up for the past three weeks, strapped down with IVs, surrounded by machines that belch and flash a sounds-and-lights symphony of her life. A birth defect ticking time bomb. Which would piss her off if she ever finds out about it, because she's a stickler for healthy eating and exercise, in better shape at sixty than most people are at twenty. After what the doctor said today, though, looks like she won't find out.

He hopes a little whiskey will loosen the words jammed up in his head, because he has to call their daughter tonight, tell her what the doctor said, maybe ask her to help him figure out what Mary would want. The bartender slaps the whiskey in place in front of him. One large ice cube clanks the edge of the glass.

If only Irv could remember the conversations they'd had about these things. He had avoided the topic of death. He couldn't imagine waking up without Mary beside him each morning. But here he's been doing it, waking up without her, for three weeks already. His first sip of whiskey burns the tightness in his throat.

The way the doctor put it was, "It's time to think of what your wife would have wanted."

"*Would* have?" Irv said.

"Yes. What she would have wanted if she could have made the choice."

As if she was dead already. He glanced toward Mary, plugged into her machines, thinking it wasn't decent to say these things in front of her.

"We can time things if you want to wait for family to join you. The process will take a few days."

The buzz of activity in the bar and the hum in his head balance out so everything around him is muffled and quiet. He doesn't notice when a woman takes the stool next to his until the bartender claps a beer in front of her. Everyone else in the place seems connected to a pair or a group, so the stool next to him was the only empty space left.

Irv lifts his glass and sniffs the fumes, takes a second bracing mouthful. If he and his daughter decide Mary wouldn't want to stay on life support, then tomorrow they'll start to ease her off, and after that it's only a matter of days. The Process.

Grace, all the way in California, had wanted to fly out right after the heart attack, but Irv asked her to wait. "You can't do anything the way things are now," he told her.

"I could keep you company."

Which was true. His life is hard and lonely right now. Work. Bedside. Work. Bedside. Laying wire in a new school in the sticks to earn money to cover hospital bills. Returning phone calls to friends asking after Mary. Repeating the same thing over and over. *I don't know. I don't know. I don't know.*

But Grace has a toddler, a baby, a job, and her husband is deployed. Irv didn't want her to come out here on an open ticket, uproot her kids for this bleary hospital existence, and risk losing her job, just so she could wait with him and feel as helpless as he does. Instead, he's been calling her every day with updates. "Status unchanged."

Tonight's call will be different.

"Cheers," the woman next to him says and raises her bottle in his direction. He lifts his own glass, as if by reflex.

After the doctor left him tonight, Irv rested his hands on his knees, then became aware of them as if they were separate from himself. He raised his eyes to take in Mary, tangled in her machines. He found her hand under the bedsheet, coaxed her fingers to unfurl and accept his.

The machine pumping Mary's air for her whooshed and sucked, whooshed and sucked. Until its noise became the sea, and Irv let himself go there. Their last anniversary, their 35th, at False Cape State Park. Mary's hand, strong and soft, in his. The long line where sea met sky, stretching out of sight. And the waves rolling in, carrying forever on their backs.

Every suck of the machine's perfect rhythm promised the opposite of forever, taking something away that it would never bring back. The first night shift nurse shuffled in, and he rose to leave like other days, ducking around her oxygen mask to kiss her cheek on his way out.

Sawed-off wine bottles dangle over the bar, makeshift light fixtures, and they cast strange circles of murky light. More students pile in, plus young couples from the neighborhood, the ones buying up all the houses and redoing everything so his and Mary's house looks shabbier by the day.

The woman beside him is at least Grace's age, or a couple years older. Thirty-something. She's pretty, but not in a fashion magazine way. Her face is squared off and powerful. She might be six feet tall. When she looks at him full on, her eyes almost knock him down. So green they remind him of phosphorescence in waves at a South Carolina beach he forgets the name of. He's only seen eyes that color on one other person. Carmen Yancey. He forces himself to look at the wood grain of the bar top instead.

If it were him in that bed in ICU instead of Mary, she wouldn't leave his side. She'd stay all night every night, regardless of any cricked neck or cramped feet or long day of work ahead. She'd bring that beanbag neck pillow she bought for their flights out to see Grace wherever her husband was stationed—Gulfport, Corpus Christi, San Diego now. She'd bring the tan and maroon afghan her Aunt Nancy crocheted for their wedding and dress up the ICU room to look halfway like home. But Irv wanders into a bar.

"I got stood up," the woman tells him. His effort at looking away must have failed, the way her comment seems like an answer to a question he hadn't asked. "Waited a whole hour at the pizza place and he never showed. Match-dot-fucking-com." She drums her fingers against the beer bottle, and her chunky rings chime against the glass.

"Must be an asshole then," he says. "Standing up a good-looking woman like you." After long weeks of not knowing what to say, it's oddly comforting to face a situation where words come easy. That same comfort, he realizes now, was at least part of what had drawn him to Carmen.

"That so?" The woman glances at him through a fall of dark curls, and her brilliant green eyes startle him all over again. Like it's Carmen herself sitting next to him, about the same age she would have been back then.

He hadn't been looking for anything when he found her, smoking on her front porch, flowery silk bathrobe shimmering in the light that spilled through the doorway behind her. For weeks after Mary delivered their first baby, Irving Junior, stillborn in his eighth month, she balled herself into the afghan on the couch, staring at the TV, eating dry cereal out of the box, not combing her hair. Irv took to walking around the city at night to see something besides his wife disappearing a little more each day.

From her porch behind a little cloud of smoke, Carmen offered him a cigarette. He said yes. To that, and more. Someone who didn't know him. Didn't know what he'd lost and wouldn't ask how he was doing today or if Mary was holding up all right. He wasn't sure if he was protecting himself or Mary more, but he never told her. And he's pretty sure she never knew.

"So you'd never pull an asshole move like that, then?" the woman says. Her eyes. Like being haunted by a living thing.

"I didn't say that. I've done my fair share of damage."

The woman belts back another swig of beer. "Yeah, good-looking man like you probably broke some hearts along the way."

Irv laughs. He minds how easy it is to laugh. Just the fleeting image of Carmen thirty years later and he lets go of everything that matters. Could he be that weak a man?

But he's not used to thinking of himself as good-looking, even though Mary always insists he looks like a movie star. Clint Eastwood. He never saw it. The best word he can come up with for the smoky image that looks back at him from the dirty mirror behind the bar is rugged. His hair long silvered, his face leathery.

He wonders what Carmen saw when she looked at him, and, for that matter, if her heart broke when he stopped coming around. All it took was Mary looking up from her sadness, one time, with him standing at the door about to walk out. She asked him not to leave, and he never went to Carmen again. Never said goodbye. When a For Rent sign popped up in her yard, he was relieved because it meant he wouldn't run into her somewhere and have to explain anything. To her or to Mary. When Grace came along two years later, the joy of that time fogged out his past with Carmen so much that, for a while, he almost believed it hadn't mattered.

He props an elbow on the bar, leans his face into his hand and rubs his temples.

"Headache?" the woman asks.

"Bigger than that," Irv says. "Much bigger."

"Hope I'm not intruding. I'm just talking to have something to do."

"I'm just drinking to have something to do." Irv taps his glass against the bar for a refill.

"The guy's Match profile said he was sensitive and reliable, if you can believe that," the woman says.

"'Loser who never shows up when he says' probably wouldn't get a lot of takers," Irv says.

"Truth." She lifts her beer bottle in his direction like tipping a hat. "How about, 'Dickwad narcissist looking for ego-stroking and fuss-free sex.' That sums up most of them." She tells him her name is Amber and that she's been sampling dating sites for a year and a half, ever since her divorce. "At least I finally found someone to buy my Doors albums and one guy gave me a free oil change, so it hasn't been a total loss."

She talks and he listens. She tells him about her dog and how he sniffs out the losers. He's been right every time. She tells him about her job managing volunteers at a senior center across town, how all the old ladies there want to fix her up with their sons or grandsons. Her steady flow of words dulls the continual loop of the doctor's words replaying in Irv's head. He sips his whiskey, orders a third, offers to buy her next beer.

"You're a good listener, Irv." She brushes her fingers against his sleeve, light as a moth landing there.

Halfway through their next drinks, more things are funny, though laughing makes Irv queasier and queasier. He needs to pay up and head out and try to make sense of the things he has to do next, but putting them off is easier.

When Irv asks for his check, Amber asks for hers too. "I don't know about you," she says, "but I'd love to keep the conversation going." That glint to her eyes adds extra meaning to her words. Even three whiskeys in, Irv feels himself harden. At that look. At the feel of her hand gently resting on his arm, waiting for his answer. At the possibility of touching someone who knows you're there.

How easy it would be to fall the same way twice. His days are a steady cycle of working, then walking the mile-plus from their house, grabbing a limp, pale-looking salad from the hospital cafeteria, and joining Mary. Every day for the better part of three weeks. Forking in a leaf of iceberg. A cherry tomato. A carrot shaving. Forcing himself to chew. While the doctors, different ones each night, start in with their questions. "Mary, can you lift your left foot for me?" Waiting, to give Mary a chance. Repeating the same questions with the right foot. Each of her hands. Asking her to open her eyes. Night after night after night.

All his salads, all the walking. Helpless acts meant to tally up and earn Mary's eyes opening again. How long has she been coaxing him to eat more vegetables? Steaming, roasting, chopping. And how many nights has he come up with excuses instead of walking with her around the neighborhood? "It's good for your heart," she always says, an irony that tastes like bile in his throat now. Her nightgown hangs on its peg on their bathroom door, making a promise it can't keep, and every night Irv stretches into their bedsheets, his toes reaching instinctively for the warmth of Mary's legs and finding nothing.

"Lord Christ," he blurts. "I can't do that, Amber."

"Jesus."

"No, I didn't mean to sound like that." He slides his empty glass away and pulls out his wallet. "At least let me treat." He pages a few bills onto the counter. "Trust me. You don't want to get mixed up with me right now."

"You know what I want now?" Amber says, her crystal eyes sharp enough to cut.

"I'm pretty sure I know what you don't want."

"So tell me, Irving. What is it I don't want?"

"For one thing, I could be your dad." Even though, with the good-time feeling drained from her face, Amber looks at least ten years older than he'd guessed, her eyes only a threat that a love child could exist.

"You're worried about your age? You look strong enough to me."

He stands from his stool. His ass aches, his legs ache. Drinking and talking took his mind off things, but his body remembers and reels with exhaustion. "It's possible, that's all I'm saying."

She lifts her beer bottle again and drains the last sip. "All you have to say is 'No thank you,' when a lady makes an offer. You don't have to go drumming up some sorry excuse. What kind of asshole does that make you?"

"That's a better question than you realize," Irv says. "Because what I'm doing here tonight drinking alone? Is figuring out what to say when I call my daughter in a few minutes to tell her her mom's dying and she needs to hop on a plane with her two kids and come say goodbye."

Amber's face loosens and her mouth falls slack. "Shit."

"Two months shy of our thirty-sixth anniversary." He squinches his eyes closed, trying to dam the tears that start falling anyway.

In the back room with the dart boards, a cheer rises up. A bull's eye. Decades he's spent wondering if Mary would've loved him anyway if she'd known about Carmen, yet all that time she had loved him. And he had loved her. For this one moment, he allows himself to think that was enough. Maybe life doesn't do bull's eyes.

"Jesus God. Look who's the asshole now," Amber says.

"Let's say nobody's the asshole." Irv dries his cheeks with the bar napkin Amber hands him. Blows his nose. "Nobody wants to be alone. It's nothing but human."

"I've been called worse."

Outside, night bugs rattle and chirp and hum, filling the darkness with life. Irv still doesn't know what to say to Grace, but his whiskeys give him courage. He dials, narrows his eyes on the moonlit sidewalk ahead. Halfway across the railroad overpass, Grace answers.

"Dad! It's so late there. Is everything okay?"

She's a mom herself now, but Irv can hear her need for her own mother in her voice. He wants to jam his thumb against the phone icon and cut the connection. He wants to thrash the phone onto the tracks, let a train rumble over it and mash it to bits. He wants one more whiskey at the bar and the sound of voices around him saying useless things. But he has a thousand things to do, and he won't be able to start a single one until he finishes telling her what she needs to know.

"Sweetheart," he says, "the doctors weren't sure before today, but they say she won't get better. It's only machines keeping her alive, and that's not what she would want."

All it took was saying the words to make him remember. If Mary could have chosen, she told him once, she would die in her sleep in the middle of a dream of swimming in the ocean. She didn't want anything to do with machines. He explains The Process to his daughter, promises it will be painless, and that she'll be able to get here in time to say goodbye. He keeps his voice soft but clear, and Grace begins to cry.

"I'm so sorry, Gracie."

"Me too, Daddy," she says. "What do we do now?"

"Just get here. I can handle the rest."

After all, he'd done it before, years ago. While Mary mucked around the house like a gray ghost of herself, Irv had called the funeral home, had met with the undertaker, had chosen their smallest casket. For the only time in their life together, she wasn't perfect either. She was no help at all, except that she insisted they buy plots for themselves beside the baby's. "We can't leave him alone in the grave-yard forever," she said, her fingers latching onto Irv's wrist. "Promise me." So she has a place to rest.

The house smells stale, like something rotting in the garbage. He ignores dirty dishes in the sink, the pile of bills on the counter, newspapers he never unrolled. He showers, shaves, puts on a comfortable striped polo and a fresh pair of jeans. He grabs a duffel bag from the cabinet beside the washing machine. It might've been Grace's from when she ran track. Aunt Nancy's afghan fits in snugly, and so does the neck pillow, his slippers. He throws in Mary's old address book for contact information that's not in his phone, and he rustles through her drawer in the bathroom to find her favorite lipstick, her mother-of-pearl comb.

This time he'll need his car, so he drives the short distance back. Parks in the garage, eerily empty at this time of night. Slings the duffel strap over his shoulder and ambles toward the soft glow of the hospital.

The doors whoosh open, but he hovers at the threshold. The strange hospital sound-mix of hush and rush lies just beyond the night air. A janitor wheeling out a trash barrel snakes around him. A security guard leaves his post inside and, curious, heads his way. Finally, Irv steps away from the doorway and sits down on a bench in the half-moon courtyard outside it.

He wants to be a good man who does the right things. He wants to get back inside, march into that elevator, and stride down the hallway to ICU, push the chair up next to Mary's bed, and hold her hand the whole night through. He wants to tuck Aunt Nancy's afghan around her, comb her hair with the mother-of-pearl comb, figure out how to put her lipstick on for her. He wants her to look nice for Gracie.

For now though, he tilts his head toward the night sky, lost in the blur of hospital lights, then closes his eyes and sees himself with Mary, walking down that False Cape beach.

Wisps of her white hair waving like sea froth on the air. Her smile, slightly wider on the right than the left, always seeming to share a joke only with him. He breathes deep and slow, and he can hear the shush-shush of the waves, the now-and-then screech of gulls. He can smell the salt in the air, feel its silt against his skin, and most of all he can feel Mary's hand clasping his, hot with life, and the sun warming their faces. Head pitched back and eyes still closed, he holds that memory of her hand, just a little longer.

Harmonie

Vanessa and Martin walked toward their favorite restaurant to meet their daughter. Julia taught middle school music in Boston, ten hours away by car, and had chosen to spend spring break across the city with her childhood best friend and her new baby. Julia had never come to town without staying with them before.

It was a cool evening in early April with a little bluster in the air, and fitful breezes crisscrossed the pedestrian mall ahead of them. They passed the corner of City Hall with its frieze of dead presidents and strode through rows of old brick buildings, all of which had been other things before the boutiques and chic eating places they were now. Once they reached the concrete basin of the fountain, stilled until summer, welcoming yellow light spilled through Harmonie's glass front.

When Julia said she'd rather meet them out than at the house, they chose Harmonie. Somehow they'd never brought her here, though it had been their favorite restaurant since the year she left for college, when they had chosen a favorite restaurant as an exercise in easing her absence. Something gained for something lost.

The hostess held the door, and another breeze whipped up behind them, scuttling a few of the year's first maple leaf seedpods inside ahead of them. Usually they made reservations, but tonight Julia had left her timing up in the air until the last minute. Henry, their regular waiter, looked happy to see them anyway. The hostess collected their coats, and Henry thumbed two menus into his hand.

"Mr. and Mrs. Langdon, always a pleasure," he said.

The best part of having a favorite restaurant was the guarantee of seeing someone who liked seeing you. "We'll be three tonight, Henry," Vanessa said.

"Will you?" Henry slid a third menu into his hands.

"Our daughter," Martin said. "Visiting from Boston."

"Visiting for the first time in a year." Vanessa strained her voice toward optimism.

"A special event then."

If she had explained how Julia wasn't staying with them, she was sure Henry would've picked up on her disappointment, but, at his suggestion, she attempted to view the dinner more as celebration than consolation. Henry pulled the chair for her, laid the menus at three of the places, and swept the fourth place setting away, all in smooth, deft gestures. As he stood again, a silver stud at a high ridge of his ear caught the light. She didn't think it had been there the last time they dined here, only two weeks ago. Reflexively, she lifted her hand to the same spot on her own ear, a place she was sure a piercing would hurt.

"We'll go ahead with our cocktails," Martin said when Henry asked if they wanted to wait for their daughter before ordering. Neither quite expected Julia to arrive on time.

A short white candle flickered at the center of every table. A detail, along with the white linen napkins and the rows of chives nestling in windowsills, that gave the place its charm. Vanessa tried to let the ambience cheer her.

Martin took her hand from across the table and laced their fingers together. "Pouting still?" Her laments had lasted from their parked car to the door of the restaurant.

"All this way and we get one dinner with her."

"It's not about us," Martin said. "If she means to help Beth with the baby, she has to be there for middle of the night wake-ups."

"But not a single night at home?" She had freshened the sheets in Julia's old room, hoping she would change her mind.

"You can't be jealous of a baby, Nessa."

But she was. Having only one child made their empty nest so definitive, and as time yawned forward, the emptiness seemed to grow. Julia's visit home without actually coming home only dramatized their obsolescence.

Outside, the twilit colors against the brick walkway reminded Vanessa of the Childe Hassam painting she had shown Julia during their June visit to Boston. For previous visits, Julia had toured them around, but last summer, Vanessa had initiated the trip to the Museum of Fine Arts, relishing the chance to share a favorite painting she remembered from Martin's days at Harvard Law when she had taken art courses at the museum. In it, a woman gazed across a snow-covered Boston Common suffused in a hazy, puce glow. Her dark, turn-of-the-last-century cloak fell to her feet. She and the two children with her seemed entranced by the white field spread before them, while streetcars and foot traffic thronged in front of a grid of buildings behind them. The painting's language of colors, shapes, and shadows communicated the kinship between mother and children along with a tangible sense of calm. A hush fell between Vanessa and Julia while they looked at it. Julia even slipped her hand through her mother's arm. For the first time in a long while, Vanessa felt they were truly seeing and experiencing the same thing.

"It's not personal," Martin said.

Determined to keep her posture from sagging with her mood, Vanessa straightened her shoulders, lifted her chin. "It's terrible advertising for parenting, though, isn't it? Becoming expendable?" She hoped she sounded more good-humored than she felt. Martin obliged her with a chuckle.

Their drinks arrived and she smiled her thanks. Henry's timing was exquisite. His ministrations at their table never felt like interruptions. Before he stepped away again, she noticed some redness around the site of his new piercing and wondered again how fresh the wound was.

Martin raised a silent toast and they took their first sips, then he faced the window, maybe searching the growing darkness for Julia.

"Seven-fifteen," Vanessa said.

"She always runs a few minutes late. You have to give her time."

"I wish she'd give us time."

At home, she would have made Julia's favorite, lemon chicken and roasted sweet potatoes with smoked paprika. She would have served ice water in the red cut-glass tumblers her grandmother had given her, wine in their best crystal. A vase of hydrangeas from the florist would have done nicely for a centerpiece. After eating, they might have played a few rounds of three-player Hearts like old times or lounged around the living room talking and sipping the cognac Martin brought out for special occasions. When everyone grew tired, they would have said their good nights and splintered into their respective rooms, leaving the warm hush of the house intact.

"I hate waiting," Vanessa said.

"Not much to like about it, I suppose." Martin braced a finger across the mouth of his glass to hold the straw in place while he took a sip from the rim. "At least we're waiting for something good."

Henry brought a basket of bread and butter, refilled their water, said nothing.

"He's so attuned to us," Vanessa said once he was out of earshot.

"He's a good sort."

"How many times do you think we've had another waiter since he started working here, Martin? Twice, maybe?"

Martin mentioned a clumsy waiter they had once. "Remember when she dropped your butter knife into your lap?" He laughed. "We never saw her after that."

"Really, though, haven't we had Henry every other time? I bet he asks for us when he sees our reservations."

"Might be," Martin said.

"He's like the son we never had." Sometimes alcohol affected her very quickly, spreading a warmth inside that radiated into her emotions.

"Not really like a son." Martin looked into his lap and adjusted his napkin there. "We don't really know him."

"But we do!" Vanessa reached across the table for Martin's wrist for emphasis and bumped the candle, splashing wax onto the tablecloth. "We probably see him more often than anyone else we know. And he's always happy to see us."

"We tip well, dear."

"Don't be such a cynic."

She rested against her seatback and took a large sip of her drink. The ice clanked when she thumped her glass down onto the table, harder than she'd meant. When Martin looked up at her, she expected a corrective expression. Instead, his eyes trained on her with gentle concern. Vanessa fumbled in her purse for lipstick, applied a fresh layer, puckered against a stray tissue, keeping her hands and gaze occupied. They had planned to have more children, but planning isn't everything. She nearly bled to death when Julia was born, and the doctor had insisted on a tubal ligation.

Their cocktails were all but drained when the door shimmered open. The reflection of the restaurant's soft light quavered with the motion of the glass, and a burst of wind rattled the silver and glassware at the few empty tables as Julia stepped inside. Martin hopped right up and strode toward her. People nearby scooted their chairs out of his way.

The only other time they'd seen her since summer had been over the holidays at Vanessa's mother's house. The rooms had teemed with Vanessa's brother and sister and their families—kids from first and second marriages—making the house feel like an arena; the visit, a spectator sport. Not a place for real connection, and Vanessa's discomfort with the chaos made her self-conscious and skittish. Julia's hair was longer now, falling loose and free to her shoulders. Her beauty always surprised Vanessa, always seemed brand new.

Martin folded Julia into a hearty hug. The force of it made them both laugh. Vanessa envied how easy they were with each other while Julia seemed to react to her as if they were magnets pushed together at the wrong ends. She lingered at the table and waited her turn, trying not to compare Julia to children she worked with as a foster care advisor who ducked out of the way when a visiting parent swooned toward them for a hug, too soon after a court-ordered separation. When Julia finally approached, she held her and counted silently to five, a time span that seemed not too clingy, before letting go again.

The hostess whisked Julia's coat from her shoulders, and Henry appeared and drew her chair for her. "Henry, this is our daughter, Julia." Vanessa's fingers brushed Julia's wrist as she spoke.

Henry clicked his heels together and nodded in almost military fashion. "Pleasure to meet you." Julia nodded in reply but didn't meet his eyes. He dismissed himself before offering her anything.

"Mother, they tell you their names because they have to. It's not personal."

Vanessa maintained a fragile smile, breathed in, then out, for another count of five. "We come here often, dear. We're regulars."

"What difference does that make?"

"He's not some random person. He knows us."

Julia flipped open her menu and Martin leaned toward her to point out a few highlights. "You can't go wrong, though. It's our favorite place," he said.

"It reminds me of Paris," Vanessa said. "A little place your father and I went on our honeymoon, near the Jardin des Tuileries."

"I bet the waiter there was Henri," Julia quipped.

Martin's startled puff of laughter disrupted Vanessa's reverie, scattering her memories of French flowers and sunshine. She smoothed the tablecloth around her bread plate. Why a meal with her daughter should make her feel so breakable she would never understand.

Henry refilled waters again, took orders, delivered Julia's cocktail, then one course of the meal at a time. Escargots, salads, mussels. They talked about Beth's baby—her shock of black hair and giant marble eyes, her tiny fingers clamping Julia's.

The pleasure Julia took in describing Beth's little girl made Vanessa wonder if she was beginning to think of babies herself. It was strange what she didn't know about her own daughter, what it seemed she wasn't welcome to ask. If Julia were in a serious relationship, she hadn't mentioned it over the phone, hadn't brought anyone with her to Grandmother's for the holidays. Vanessa would have to take those omissions as answers. For now, she was left to picture herself in a rocking chair, holding a hypothetical future grandchild to her chest, stroking its warm head, inhaling that fragrance of fresh-bathed baby hair. She would have to trust that such a time would come, and, when it did, that Julia would share it with her.

"What are you thinking, Mother?"

Worried her silence seemed calculated, Vanessa mustered a polite question. "How is Beth adjusting to motherhood?"

Julia answered with an odd anecdote about the first outing Beth and her husband had taken the baby to, a friend's party. She had slept through the whole thing, strapped into her car seat carrier. Beth and her husband took turns carting her from room to room, catching up with people they hadn't seen since the baby was born.

"All night they'd been telling everyone what an easy baby she was, so easy they hardly knew she was there," Julia said. "Then they buckled themselves all the way into their car in the driveway before they realized they'd left her inside!"

Vanessa gave a quick, uneasy laugh while Martin scooped the last escargot from its shell.

"They hardly knew she was there all right," Julia said. To her it was the end of a funny story, but too many stories from Vanessa's work started similar ways. She couldn't help but picture that little baby, left behind, blinking in a room full of strangers.

"Beth had nightmares afterward, that they got all the way home without her and the police took her away. Parenthood changes you. That's what Beth says."

"Of course it does!" Vanessa reached toward her daughter's hand. Julia cupped her water glass instead of reaching back.

Martin sopped leftover juice from the escargot platter with a corner of bread. "So you've caught us up on Beth. How about you?"

Vanessa marked Julia's expression at the question, the same uncertain look that once preceded admissions of childhood guilt—a vase broken, a homework assignment forgotten—but the bustle of people leaving the next table cut Julia off before she could answer. The hostess and one of the other waiters delivered coats, leading to a flurry of arms seeking armholes, shuffling feet, and laughter as people knocked into each other and into the tables, accidentally scooting them across the slippery tiles. The last to leave was a tipsy woman wearing too much red lipstick who stumbled against the back of Vanessa's chair on her way toward the door. She leaned over and breathed a garlic-laced, "Excuse us," into Vanessa's face.

A moment later, something strange in the cluster of abandoned dishes at the just-emptied table caught Vanessa's attention. Flames shot up two or three inches from a napkin left too near one of the candles. Calling for help would slow the response, so Vanessa leapt from her chair with her own napkin poised in the air and clapped it down on top of the burning one.

"Nicely done, Nessa!" Martin began soft applause, and other diners followed the cue. Her success made her draw in a self-conscious laugh.

"I didn't know what to think when you jumped up," Julia said after Vanessa sat down again. "You looked like you were about to run away."

Vanessa smiled, pleased to have caught Julia's interest. "But I didn't mean to steal your spotlight. You were getting ready to tell us how you've been."

"I've been quite well, actually."

And she did look well. Her color was good, for one thing. Boston winters often kept her too much indoors and, by this time of year, she seemed pasty and waifish.

"Good, good. So you're still enjoying your job?" Vanessa said.

"That's something I wanted to talk to you about," she said, and all that good color drained away. Vanessa realized she couldn't recall the last time Julia had mentioned anything specific about her students, and she couldn't imagine what they had talked about instead.

Henry gave a soft cough to announce his presence and lowered a platter of chocolate-drizzled profiteroles in front of her. "For saving the day," he said. "On the house." Piped in chocolate along the plate's border: "Our hero."

"How sweet, Henry," she said. He winked and retreated with their dirty dishes. The hostess dealt dessert plates and spoons then vanished as well.

Vanessa basked in her moment and served everyone from the platter. "There I go stealing the spotlight again," she said. Then, to Julia, "But let's get back to hearing about your life."

"Ahh, my life." Julia took a long sip from her water glass. "The truth is, I resigned after winter term."

The serving spoon still hovered in Vanessa's hand. "Without mentioning it? In all the times we've talked since then?" She glanced at Martin who looked equally dumbstruck, then lowered the spoon, where the words on the platter had already smeared.

"I wanted to believe I was inspiring artists the way my middle school music teacher had inspired me," Julia said.

Vanessa nodded emphatically. "Inspiring artists is a noble calling. And teaching is a stable career. Not every musician gets both."

"True." Julia seemed to examine the morsel of pastry on her spoon, then set it back on her plate. "But the kids deserve someone who loves the teaching as much as the music."

"But you do love teaching," Vanessa said.

"I *liked* teaching. But it didn't fit me."

"I don't understand, though, dear. What will you do for money?"

Martin placed a hand across Vanessa's wrist, an old gesture meant to slow her down. "You must have new plans then," he said.

"I do." She gazed at each of them in turn, as if she were measuring them in some way. "I'm in a band with some friends. We've been playing nights at a bar in Boston off and on for a few years."

"A bar?" Vanessa said.

"Not just a bar. More of a music venue. Last spring and summer we put a bunch of our stuff up on YouTube, and we started getting calls for gigs from all over—some as far as New York City. It got rough getting up to teach in the mornings with all the late nights and long drives, so I had to make some tough decisions."

"Tough, yes," Vanessa said. They each took another bite of dessert. Vanessa's had the mouthfeel of cardboard. "I thought you'd outgrown your garage band days." The tone of her own voice made her cringe. She hurried her next spoonful to keep her mouth too full to say more.

"We're not goofing around," Julia said. "We're serious musicians." She planted her chin on top of steepled hands, as if she were praying for them to understand her, and Vanessa wanted to understand.

Henry arrived at the table to offer coffee, seeming aware of their need for some kind of break. Julia ignored him; Martin nodded for espresso; Vanessa shook her head.

"There are four of us. We call ourselves the Nuclear Sunset Experiment." For this part, Julia kept her head down and plowed her spoon in circles around her plate. Melted ice cream and profiterole fragments puddled into the designs she made. "I'm the lead singer."

"I've always loved your voice," Vanessa said, and Julia smiled at her for the first time all evening. When Vanessa reached for her daughter's hand this time, Julia finally allowed her to hold it.

"You can check us out on YouTube if you want." She sounded so hopeful. "I'm doing temp work in Boston and some bartending. Both good paying jobs that I can work around my gig schedule. My bandmates and I even went in on an apartment together to save on rent. We move in next week."

Vanessa winced at this detail. She'd loved the little Victorian Julia had rented with another teacher, a few short miles from the school where they taught. The cozy sofabed for guests, its sheets sprinkled with tiny sprays of pink roses, matching the rose-shaped soaps in the bathroom. The photo on the side table from their family trip to the Grand Canyon when Julia was twelve. She and Martin flanked the snout of the mule, and Julia sat gawkily atop it. Her elbows poked out to the sides and her teeth seemed too large for her grin. How Vanessa missed the girl from that picture, her body as spiky as her moods had been, yet she still knocked on their bedroom door for nightmares.

"And you can go back to teaching, when you're finished traveling around," Vanessa said as the thought occurred to her. "As long as you keep your certification current, right?"

Julia's already tentative smile shrank back into itself.

"What's wrong with keeping your certification?" Vanessa looked from Julia to Martin before Henry materialized and set Martin's espresso on the table. Martin framed his hands around the saucer but otherwise paid no attention to it.

"I'm not going to keep my certification current," Julia said when Henry was gone. "I don't know if we'll even stay in the States. We might go to Europe."

"Europe?" The distance from home, the vastness of the planet made Vanessa feel small.

Martin's forehead crimped in seeming sympathy with her. His chair squeaked as he leaned forward. "You have a right to do whatever you please, of course," he said, ever the diplomat. "But you must understand what a surprise this is. Such a big change. No more health insurance. No retirement."

"No, Dad. No safety net."

No place for us to stay when we visit, Vanessa didn't say. An apartment crammed with bandmates would have no room for a sofabed, that Grand Canyon picture, the little rose soaps. She imagined the space cluttered with instruments and dirty clothes, small dishes of cigarette butts and ash, empty and half-empty beer cans littering windowsills and countertops. Twenty steps backwards from the stability and hominess of her last place.

"It all seems so sudden and drastic," said Vanessa.

"This isn't a tragedy," Julia said. "I'm happy now. I wasn't before."

"You never said." Julia's hand slipped from hers, and Vanessa couldn't keep herself from arguing. "Anyway happiness isn't a permanent condition. People think it is these days, but it's only ever peak moments of lifetimes. Short bursts. Nobody's happy all the time."

"Would you advise me against trying to be happier?" She seemed to strangle the napkin in her lap.

"I'd advise you to act reasonably," Vanessa said.

"When have I been anything but reasonable? I've never asked for help or money or anything else." Her chair scraped the tiles as she stood and gestured for her coat. "You always want to solve problems I don't have."

"Please, don't go," Martin said, standing and clasping her hand.

"You're ashamed of me."

Martin looked helpless. "Of course I'm not," he said, but he had hesitated. Julia shook her hand free and tilted her head away so she wouldn't have to look at them on her way outside. Another rush of air blasted across the room as the door swung shut behind her, snuffing their candle and leaving Vanessa to shiver in her seat. Martin stood by the table, one hand on the back of his chair, the other still stretched toward where Julia had been moments ago. Vanessa could tell he was weighing whether he should race after her. She had never seen him second-guess himself before.

Martin finally eased back into his seat. Henry uncorked a wine bottle at the next table. Somewhere a cell phone rang.

Of course Julia had a right to do as she pleased, just like Martin said. That didn't make it easy to watch. No matter how beautiful, how rare you were, the world could swallow you whole.

Eventually Martin dropped the sugar cube into his espresso and stirred. The clatter of it irked Vanessa. There would always be more cups of coffee, more meals, more nights out, just the two of them. Julia farther and farther away.

At his next stop at the table, Henry said, "You have a lovely daughter. You must be so proud."

Martin refolded the napkin from his lap and laid it on the table in front of him. "They go their own way, you know."

Hugging herself against the last of the chill, Vanessa struggled to zero in on Henry, then narrowed her focus around his ear. "Did it hurt?" she asked, touching her own ear again. "It seems like such a tender spot."

"It is." Henry crossed one foot behind the opposite ankle, sank his hip a little. "But it didn't hurt for long. Just a pinch. A really hard pinch, then it was over."

"That's good," Vanessa said. "Good it didn't hurt for long."

Henry leaned toward the table confidingly. "I was afraid they wouldn't want me to wear it to work, but they haven't said a word."

"You must not be free to do as you please at a job like this," Vanessa said, realizing it for the first time. "But do you like it, Henry?"

"I do," he said. "The atmosphere. People like you."

He was such a nice young man.

"Henry? I have a crazy idea." Vanessa pressed her hands together in front of her. Martin eyed her quickly, maybe surprised she would share a crazy idea with Henry before suggesting it to him first. "All these years you've been waiting on our table. What if you come to our house? Let us wait on *you* for a change. Next week maybe. What's your day off?" In her mind, she was already arranging the red tumblers, the vase of hydrangeas. Behind his napkin, Martin cleared his throat with the sound of an engine starting.

"My day off?" Henry uncrossed his ankles and cast a worried glance over his shoulder. "I'm not sure…I don't think management would like that idea." His excuse built itself word by word until he seemed comfortable with it, then he mixed a nod with a shrug, an apology, as if any of them believed the decision hadn't been his to make. In his rush back toward the kitchen, he stubbed into a table leg and nearly lost his balance.

The hostess placed the bill on the table without a word. Normally, Martin would pay with a credit card, but tonight he counted off twenties and ones. The hostess breezed back to the table with their coats. Martin cradled Vanessa's elbow and escorted her outside. The crisp air had turned much colder by now, and the car seemed miles away.

Martin braced an arm around her shoulders as they walked. The wind had picked up and clouds obscured the starlight. Mostly bare branches creaked in the wind. An alley they passed reeked of garbage and urine. People around them turned wavy as tears clouded Vanessa's eyes.

"It's not like he had to say yes," she said.

"He certainly could have said thank you," Martin said. "A thank you was in order."

Closer to their car, they walked under a streetlamp whose light had burnt out. Martin opened Vanessa's door and held it for her. Before he started the car, he looked long at her, as if checking for visible wounds.

"We'll find a new restaurant," he said. "A new favorite."

She pictured the next restaurant where all the waiters were strangers, not one happy to see them, and she saw their future mapped out in favorites, one lost, another gained, one lost again, until the long distant end of their lives.

Things Are Already Better Someplace Else

All you did was use the toilet. Then clear away the blocks Beverly had left scattered in the entryway. You didn't want anyone to trip later, coming inside. You left her with her sidewalk chalk out in front of the duplex. Singing one of her wordless songs. Silence was your first clue, even before you recognized the car swerving off down the road.

Your Beverly is a smudge of a child. A shadow of herself, but powdery pale so she catches what light there is and shimmers in it. When her daddy pulled up to the curb, she must have figured he wouldn't see her. When was Mickey ever looking for her? She's his own child, but you have to force him to watch her nights you work late. Daytimes there's the cheap daycare down the road, but his mama's your only other choice for nights, and she won't say yes unless you ask him first.

At least she lives close to him. One of the million reasons your marriage didn't last past squat, but for Beverly she gives a damn, and she's never drunk or dangerous like Mickey. She might return Beverly to you, reeking of soap she bought from some fancy store at the mall, that smug smile saying she judged you never bathed her on your own. Because you use unscented soap. The only kind that doesn't pock her skin into hives. Whenever old witchy Wilma drops

Beverly back off, you have to plop her in a warm water bath first thing, to soak those perfumey soaps off her, stop the hives before they pop.

At least she doesn't ignore the child the way Mickey does. Sometimes Beverly eats dry cereal for supper by herself at his place. When her daddy finally rolls in from a friend's house two doors down or the bar across the street, she pretends to be asleep instead of hungry since half the time he cooks for her he forgets, walks away from the pan until something catches fire. You've told her, just go down to Granny Wilma's if he's not there to feed you dinner or if he walks off with a pan on the stove, but Beverly shakes her tiny little head with the wisdom of a ghost and lets you wonder why. If you had anywhere else to send her, you would. You wish you could send her straight to Wilma, even though she seethes when you call her on the phone.

You have to call her now, though, because that was Mickey's car squealing away from the curb, and now Beverly's nowhere to be found. Every last stalk of sidewalk chalk lies tiddlywinks by the curb. Her half-empty juice box sits by the pile, waiting as much as you for the child to slink back into view.

Wilma says into the phone she hasn't seen Mickey since yesterday and her voice has the crisp sound of something about to break. She knows you wouldn't call after him in all your life if not for Beverly. Knows he doesn't pay support, and you don't have enough food. Knows he doesn't do you a single bit of good. Out of some warped brand of loyalty, she still blames you for starting the fights, before and after you left. You've seen her fill a doorway to stop him from barreling through it, though. To stop him from barreling smack into you. Sure, she spits your name like a thing caught in her teeth. Thinks you grew out of a mud pit with manners you'd expect of a pig. Well fuck her, but thank God for her too. Probably resents you most for not leaving sooner. She begot a monster and blames you for waking it, for keeping it awake.

Beverly's no monster, though. A breath of wind, she is. A breath of wind with the scent of honeysuckle on it. A breath of wind and a little bird song. And after her daddy's car tore off up the street, she's gone.

"Wilma, he took her," you say.

"What do you know? You always think the worst."

"I got good reason."

"Yeah, well."

"I saw him, Wilma. I saw his car, and then she was gone."

"When was this?"

"Just five minutes ago."

The line itself seems to hum or stutter, then, "Probably she just ran and hid when he pulled up."

She does tend to fade in and out of a scene. Hears her daddy coming and glides behind the phone pole out front, leans into it as if she's part of it, and he stomps past her, shouting your name, and his latest string of fuck yous and all the dumbass things he thinks you've done to make him look bad. How it's your fault his latest boss let him go. Your fault his best friend never comes by to see him anymore. Your fault the neighbors shrink back from him like he's walking roadkill. You haven't seen the people he accuses you of turning against him since your last fight that day you finally braced Beverly to your chest, packed two grocery bags full of her clothes, and walked out. The two of you slept on the sofa in your friend Nathan's basement apartment for a full month until your face healed and you could go out looking for the next job.

"Ran off like she always does, baby," Wilma says. "She always hides from her daddy." She never calls you baby unless she's scared. Once, at the hospital, you woke to Wilma begging you, *Please, please, please, baby, wake up. Wake up again, baby,* and also, *Please, please, please, God, take his daddy out of him,* letting you picture her, in some past time, with somebody sitting by her bedside, praying she'd wake up.

You tell her about the chalk and the juice box and the sweep of wind that rolled up the hillside after the car was gone. The cold sweep of wind that pricked goosebumps up your arms.

"Don't go thinking that way now," she says.

You call the police, and a car zips up the street with siren lights circling, circling like buzzards, and you don't want to think that way, either. They ask you questions. Where he might go. What he might do. Like you would've called them if you already knew.

They ask if you have a protective order, and you try to explain the divorce documents. By the time you made it official, Beverly was almost three years old and you were still learning how to juggle the job at the Citgo Shop & Go plus two nights a week tending bar at the Funky Monkey down by the railroad tracks. You downloaded something online and met once with lawyers at a legal aid clinic. You couldn't afford anything more complicated, but it's all set up so he's only allowed to have Beverly when you're at work.

"Why does he babysit for her if he's so dangerous?" one asks, poking his holstered hip your way and staring down his nose like Wilma does.

"It ain't babysitting when it's your own kid. She's his kid." You tell them Wilma goes over there any time she can, but she works at the post office, sorting mail, evenings sometimes, mornings. She can't always be there the whole time.

They ask, "Where were you when it happened?"

"Bathroom. For one second."

You used the toilet, swooshed the blocks out of the doorway, but you don't tell them how you thought about stretching onto the sofa to claim five seconds of your own time, tired from the late shift the night before and the trouble Mickey gave you after, for wrangling Beverly out of his house to sleep in her own real bed and not wedged into his bristly cigarette-stinking sofa cushions. But you didn't sit down, only rushed back out to the yard in time to notice the silence and glimpse Mickey's car disappearing in the cloud of dust it kicked up going so fast.

"What happened lately that he might be angry about?" Like Wilma, *What'd you do this time?*

"That man is angry all the time."

They ask, "Why not just schedule your hours so you and Wilma can share?"

"You get to pick what hours you work? And are you writing anything down? That bastard took my daughter. Are you gonna stop asking me questions and go look for her?"

Because you can't tell if they plan to do more than pride themselves on knowing what's happening to you could never happen to one of them. How they're too upstanding and kind-hearted to be such a twat to their women, or their women are tougher than you and wouldn't take that kind of shit anyway. Well, you don't know what you'll take until you survive it, do you?

Feels like a hundred hours they stand there asking questions, and it's like all of you are swimming in molasses. One officer flips his card into your hand so you can call if Mickey turns up again.

"*If* he turns up again? What do you think's gonna happen?" They give you statue faces and drive away.

She's been gone five minutes, ten minutes, five hours. Cell phones across America screech out warnings and descriptions of Mickey's car and of your little girl and her unicorn t-shirt with the SpaghettiOs stain at the edge of the pale blue neckline. Her blue sneakers and white ankle socks. How her tiny fingernails are flecked with pink polish, only a few tattered strips of it leftover.

You picture your bosses and neighbors and people you work with hearing the warning and ignoring it, figuring it's no one they know, nothing they can do. You picture Beverly in the back seat of Mickey's decrepit Mustang flying past their ignorant windows, face and hands pressed to the glass, wishing with all her might to be back at the sidewalk, scraping chalk rainbows onto the cement, her mama beside her.

What else can you do but pace the house, inside and outside. Drum your fingers on your thighs, your temples, the kitchen counter. You page through texts on your phone for one you might've missed. The police said let them handle it, they'd do all they could, whatever that might be, and night's coming on and Beverly needs her supper and a warm bath with the unscented soap, and you picture those sickly fake cherry-scented soaps in gas station bathrooms, and how far will he go? Where can he go?

The knock on the door lifts your spirits so high your whole body follows. Thinking it'll be one of the police officers holding Beverly by the hand. Shook up and tearstained but whole and home. But it's Wilma, looking ragged and sleep-wrecked, as if it's been ten days already instead of six or seven hours.

You step outside, waiting for her to blame you. To say, *You know he don't like you questioning his parenting. You challenge him on something and it's just the same to him if he proves you right or wrong. He's gonna prove something, either way,* and that's why, according to Wilma, everything you've ever said to him is wrong.

You pool up all your patience to look her in the eye. Bottom line, Beverly's hers too, and just as gone from her as she is from you. You sit down on the front stoop and pat the space beside you.

It's a warm night, before mosquito season. Darkness fell when you weren't looking and now stars blink through the blackness, reporting some kind of message from a zillion miles away. Maybe, *Things get better.* Maybe, *Things are already better someplace else.* Maybe, *You're just a speck of dust on the back of the world and nothing really matters anyway.* On a good night, they tell you, *Everything's a star that shines. You're a star that shines. Your little girl, the brightest star of all.*

Now Wilma sits beside you, body rigid as live wires. She's never been one to soften, even for Beverly. She laughs with her, a smoker's rasp, and rolls a ball her way. Buys her little teddy bears with velvet hearts sewn on. But her body stays stiff, vigilant. You hope you won't be the same way, twenty years past Mickey. You hope your body forgets how to steel itself for a blow.

"You think he means to come back?" she asks, with you hoping to hear she was sure he was already on his way. Hoping she'd tell you, *He's done a load of stupid shit but wouldn't hurt Beverly for the world.* It would've comforted you no matter if she'd used her meanest voice and said again, *The only girl he ever hit was you.* At least it's true he's never hit Beverly.

"I don't know," you say, and your head bowls forward in your hands. Sobs ratchet out of you and you think Mickey would throw back his head and cackle if he could see you, sharing a step with his mama, expecting she had more feelings than a fish washed up on shore. *My mama's a cold ass bitch*, he told you, same day he mentioned seeing his daddy knock her unconscious when he was a kid. She woke up bleeding from her forehead and went after the man with a hatchet. Dropped it long before she caught up to him, but still Mickey won't forgive her.

Wilma inches closer and frames an arm behind you. "We'll get her back," she says. She repeats it a few times, and by the last time she's certain. "We'll get her back, and that motherfucker won't see her again."

You let Wilma rub circles onto your back. Let yourself believe her. You don't care if she calls you ditch-trash again or blames you next time Beverly brings head lice home from daycare or if she never listens about what kind of soap Beverly's skin can manage. You cry until the tears run dry, and hope in the end the two of you can stay as strong and angry as it takes to keep him away.

If you're lucky enough, this one time, for him to come back.

The Secret Life of Otto and Hilda

Otto Augsburg knew exactly what he wanted when he walked into the Jiffy-J on Avon Street. Utz sour cream and onion potato chips, his favorite American junk food. Actually, the chips were the only American junk food Otto ate, and the Jiffy-J was the only store in town that carried them. He knew because he owned office buildings and other business concerns in nearly every area of town, giving him the chance to explore most local convenience stores and keep track of who stocked them.

He purchased the single serving size, the bag no longer than the fingers of his own hand, because that was always enough to slake his craving. He would have bought the bag and gone on his way today without anything of interest happening if one more thing, standing at the checkout counter, hadn't caught his attention and set off an entirely new craving. The bright red human-height plastic M&M, with black plastic arms and legs, white mitts for hands, white boots for feet, wearing a Christmas hat and a smirk. Otto wanted that too.

Unlike some of his colleagues, who bought Jaguars for their children's sixteenth birthdays or vacation homes in Jamaica, Otto preferred more modest indulgences. Especially ones that tickled his sense of humor. Here—this thing was ridiculous: If one wished for candy, why would one be likelier to buy it at the hands of a giant, anthropomorphic morsel of it? A Santa Claus hat, four full months after the holiday had passed, added spice to the silliness.

He would buy it and give it to his daughter, now in her third year at UVA. Surely Marta would enjoy the absurdity as much as he did. Anyone would. And a surprise like this one justified a spontaneous visit, even though she discouraged these. What he considered a German propensity for timeliness and propriety skipped him, more or less, but manifested itself perfectly in Marta. She was stern and precise in her habits, particularly as they regarded spending time with him. He was always looking for a way around her reserve.

At least she still talked to him. She was the only child of his second marriage, and his two children from his first marriage, now in their thirties, lived in California and Montana and only called a couple times a year. Otherwise, they didn't seem to think of him, except when they wanted money. Same with both ex-wives.

Otto laid his chips on the counter, and the clerk looked up at him over the steaming brim of a Styrofoam cup. He wore a striped polo shirt under a red apron stamped with Jiffy-J in white letters. He scanned the bag with the register wand. "Anything else?"

"In fact there is." Otto fished for proper phrasing. Even after forty years in the States, American consumer culture still amused him, but his humor didn't always translate. He opted for the simplest words possible. "How much for that?" he asked, motioning toward the life-sized M&M.

Strapped to the M&M was a tray of small bags of the candy: dark chocolate, milk chocolate, peanut, pretzel. The clerk pointed to the sign that hung from it. "Three for a dollar."

"No, not that." Otto let out a soft laugh. The clerk couldn't know that any candy Otto ate was shipped directly from his homeland. "The creature."

"Creature?" the clerk answered, startled. He shot looks over both shoulders before settling his gaze on the M&M. "You mean *that*? Sounded like some kinda horror movie thing."

"Yes," Otto said, touching the M&M's ersatz shoulder. "This fellow, right here." He imagined Marta's face when he brought it to her later, how her usual focused, determined expression would give way to something softer and easier.

"Not for sale."

The odor of hot dogs rotating in a case behind the man began to disturb Otto. Long, skinny, pinkish tubes revolved in the brash orange light of the countertop heating oven. Such a poor imitation of actual frankfurters. Otto caught his own reflection, distorted in the chrome housing of the oven, his wild whorls of white hair and bushy eyebrows meeting in the middle, his face drawn long and rippling like in a funhouse mirror. Not for the first time, he wondered how other people saw him.

"It's well past the holidays." Otto tapped one of his long, thin fingers against the fringe of the Santa hat.

"Don't matter."

"What will happen to it, though?" Otto asked. "Surely someone will collapse this display? Heave the creature into the garbage? Any day now."

The clerk picked up his coffee cup again and took another sip. "I wouldn't know," he said. "Buck fifty for the chips."

"Must be worth something." Otto was not one to back away from a deal.

"It just ain't something we sell, man," the clerk said. "Don't know what else to tell you."

Once when Marta was small, Otto brought her a mason jar full of tadpoles from a friend's pond. Tiny writhing things tumbled in the murky pond water, endlessly entertaining to watch. And his friend had called them "pollywogs," a source of hilarity on its own. Marta took the jar with a look of trust in him and wonder at the world. With every gift he's given her since, he's hoped to reproduce that reaction.

"Everything's for sale, young man," Otto said. "And just look at him, with his little Santa cap. Clearly whoever brought him here has forgotten about him now that we're in the month of April." He pulled a roll of cash from his pants pocket. "It's a question, I suppose, of what it's worth to you."

"I don't own the place," the clerk said, flustered. "I mean, hell, I'd love to take your money, but…"

Otto leafed several bills, all fifties, off the roll. "How about these? Will these cover it?" he said, handing over the stack of cash that now curled together, making a roll of its own. "Share it with your boss. Then everybody's happy, yes?"

The clerk didn't argue. Satisfied, Otto unhitched the tray of M&Ms and its cardboard shoulder-strap from the creature, then tossed another $1.50 onto the counter. "For the chips," he said and slipped the little bag into his rumpled blazer pocket before bracing the M&M and wrangling it out the door of the Jiffy-J.

Outside, Otto leaned the creature upright for a moment so he could zap his key remote to unlock his bullet-shiny Mercedes-Benz and open the passenger door. Then he tried to slide the M&M into the passenger seat, pushing from the rounded shoulders, but it didn't bend into a sitting position and swiveled the wrong direction instead, bumping against the open door. Next, Otto laced his arms around its broad waist and sat in the seat himself, pulling the M&M onto his lap. It remained rigid, but this method succeeded. He slid out from under it and went around to the driver's side, waved to the clerk through the glass storefront, and got in.

Before he could take the M&M to Marta, Otto had meetings to attend and business errands to accomplish. When he emerged from a banking appointment downtown, a man with a small dog stood beside Otto's car, staring into it.

"That's old Hilda," he said, conjuring the name in that instant, because it seemed funnier and better for the creature to have a name that had nothing to do with its American branding. The display at the store had pegged this creature as male, but the sudden name also came with Hilda's decided femaleness. She was a hearty, laughing sort of woman. Maybe because of the hat, he pictured her around a fireplace at an Alpine ski lodge, telling loud stories to an appreciative audience of fellow skiers. "She likes jokes."

The man with the dog smiled now that he could tell Otto didn't mind his peering into the car. The dog's claws scrabbled the sidewalk as Otto eased open his door. "Dirty jokes best of all," he said to the man, offering a two-fingered salute before sinking into the driver's seat again. Out of his rearview he watched the man shake his head and walk away. "How about that, Hilda?" he said. "People can't keep their eyes off of you."

Next came a meeting of his development group, reviewing plans to turn a derelict warehouse into office space downtown. He loved the power of transforming wasted space into something beautiful and new. He left the meeting tossing his keys into the air and catching them, whistling a happy tune as a light rain thrummed around him.

It was a pizza delivery woman ogling Hilda this time, using the vinyl pizza pouch as an umbrella. When Otto approached, she lifted her head. "You got yourself some good company there."

"She never gets tired of me," Otto said. They both laughed.

Now that it was rush hour, Otto traveled the most congested intersections on purpose, in order to get caught at stoplights. This afforded him more chances to watch people react to Hilda before he gave her away. At one light, he fetched a paper napkin out of his glove compartment and carefully daubed Hilda's face. A woman in the next lane flinched and turned away as if he had done something obscene.

The line of traffic was so long, Otto had to stop at the same light again, and this time he pretended to argue with Hilda, mouthing no real words but pinching his eyebrows together and shaking one fist in the air toward her. The guy in the left turn lane beside him shot disgusted looks in his direction and kept creeping forward, edging farther away from him.

For Otto's last trick, he leaned over and pretended to give Hilda a full-on mouth kiss, a long slow one. When he opened his eyes again, the light had turned green. The driver behind him laid on his horn. Otto laughed and waved into his rearview, as if the man could share the joke.

By now, copper sunlight crested the blue mountain ridges and edged the trailing strands of the day's clouds with a metallic sheen. Dogwoods bloomed and redbud blossoms feathered through the air. He wasn't far from Marta's apartment now, at a red light at Cherry and Ridge. It was a good time of day, past afternoon classes and before evening ones. He wouldn't be interrupting. Never mind her frequent reminders to plan his visits ahead. Meeting Hilda deserved an element of surprise.

"Hilda, liebling, I've got someone I'd like you to meet." Otto's voice boomed in the tight space. He was surprised how much he enjoyed her company, how the bright flash of red never quite stopped being funny to him. "What's that you say? Better than some old pollywogs?" He craned toward her with a hand against his ear, as if to listen better. "I couldn't agree more."

He would miss her when she was gone, but Marta would have such fun with her. She'd make a ridiculous prop for parties or a great gag to play on a friend. You could make her knock on somebody's door, tuck her into somebody's bed, bring her to class.

He turned into Marta's apartment building's parking lot and pulled into one of the spaces marked GUEST. He had offered to buy Marta a little house even closer to Grounds, but she had said no. She worked at a coffee shop and paid her own bills. A scholarship paid her tuition. He appreciated her self-sufficiency, but he regretted not being allowed to spoil her. She wouldn't even let him pay for a parking spot for her in the university lot. She claimed she preferred to walk.

Hilda's hard plastic shell plunked against the door as Otto wrestled her out of the car. It was drizzling again, and rain made her slippery. He carried her piggyback, holding her by the tops of her legs, her stiff body jutting upright at an angle from his. She was heavier than he had gauged from his first moments transferring her into the car. A couple times along the sidewalk he had to stop to catch his breath and mop sweat off his face with his lavender-scented handkerchief.

Other students who lived in the same building trickled in from different directions with backpacks slung over one shoulder. Some said hi to him and Hilda. Others pointed from afar and laughed. Everyone looked. Otto took the attention as a sign of his success and imagined news of his gift circulating out among the university's thousands of students. He believed certain things to be as true for others as for himself, and he felt anyone who had thought of it would have wanted to take the creature from the store. What made him special a lot of the time, in life the same as in business, was that when he saw something he wanted he went for it. People understood the wanting, and they envied his ability at the getting.

Otto half-dragged, half-carried Hilda up every flight of the outdoor staircase to his daughter's third floor apartment. At Marta's door, he stood Hilda up just beyond view of the peephole, poofed his hair with his fingers, and wiped his forehead with his handkerchief one more time. Hilda was sprinkled with raindrops from their walk, so he patted her dry as well. The hallway was brightly lit, and Hilda gleamed. He chuckled into his hand, then knocked.

His daughter's roommate was South Korean, with a name that sounded like Hi. Even after spending his entire adult life in America, Otto was self-conscious about how the remnants of his accent prevented him from matching Marta's instructions for pronouncing the girl's name. He preferred not to say it all. Marta noticed how he avoided using her name and frowned at him when it happened.

When the doorknob rattled, sticking a little, he pictured Marta's roommate on the other side with her perennial tie-dyed t-shirts and spray of forehead acne. But when the door opened, he was relieved to see Marta instead. She wore sweatpants and her wire-rimmed reading glasses. She bought most of her clothes from Goodwill, instead of letting him buy her attractive new clothes, and he was pretty sure she'd used the same glasses since middle school.

Most of her blond hair was swept into a ponytail, except for the bangs and some soft strands that had gotten tired from being held so tight and had drifted free. She looked tired herself and showed no signs of joy when she looked at him. At sight of Hilda, she made an audible exhale, then steeled her expression, the way her mother had those last years before the divorce.

"Voilà!" Otto said, presenting Hilda with a grand swoop of his hands.

"What is this?" Marta crossed her arms. One hand held a pencil, and it spiked out and away from her like a tiny saber. She looked from Hilda to her father. She didn't step away from the threshold or make any motion to let him in.

"Great for parties. A gag gift? A practical joke?"

Marta didn't even smile.

"I thought you'd like it." Otto could hear the sadness in his own words.

"You thought I'd like a giant M&M?"

"I did, really." Otto's smile felt crooked. He almost touched it to check its symmetry.

Marta's next expression was a ringer for another of her mother's. Equal parts exasperation and pity. "It doesn't look like something I'd want. Look at it, Dad. It's all you."

Something inside him smarted. He did look at Hilda, but he wasn't sure what Marta thought he would see.

"I hope you didn't pull one of your money tricks to get it?"

"Money tricks?" Otto noticed that Marta's feet were bare and her toenails needed a trim. A few thin strips of old polish clung along the nails, and the edges were split and rough.

"Nobody just sells stuff like that," she said. "I bet you threw a bunch of cash at some unsuspecting kid who didn't have a right to say yes or the will to say no. Just like that time at your club."

He had taken her out to dinner at his country club many times, but she was talking about something that happened in the fall. The glass-walled dining room overlooked the club's golf course. A rugged backdrop of Blue Ridge foothills, afire with fall colors, framed the manicured greens, a perfect contrast of wild and tame. "I just wanted my usual table."

"So you paid the waiter-kid to move a family who was already sitting there." Marta sounded more puzzled than angry, but her words put Otto on edge.

"I bought them champagne for the trouble. They seemed happy enough." His voice had risen, but he quieted it again. Footsteps sounded down the hall, and he didn't want anyone to see him, stuck in the hallway with the huge M&M and a daughter who wouldn't let him into her apartment.

"I know, I know. The best champagne in the wine cellar, and your fluttering waves of thanks." Marta mimicked his gesture from that night with a tired look on her face. "But what difference would it have made for us to sit somewhere else? We would've seen the sunset just as well one table over."

The footsteps faded, then began echoing from a stairwell. Still, Otto felt embarrassed. He wanted to remind Marta that the hostess was the one who had made the mistake. He had booked his usual table beside the window, and he'd felt generous paying someone else to correct the error. Generous again when he'd made things right with the family that had moved. But there was truth in Marta's words that he didn't fully grasp, and he knew she wouldn't let go of her argument.

"Anyway, I'm in the middle of writing a paper. Due tomorrow," she said. "That's why I always ask you to call before you come by. I don't have time for random visits."

"I just wanted to bring you a gift." His tone shifted. She seemed only to see him for his blunders. Two weeks after he'd given her that jar of pollywogs, she brought it back to him, every tadpole floating belly up, not one left to turn into a frog. The look she gave him then was full of blame and sorrow, feelings that seemed to shadow every look she's given him since.

No matter how hard he tried. He had gone to some lengths to acquire Hilda today, and he wanted, maybe, just a simple thank you. A shred of appreciation.

"You know, Dad, just one time I'd love to get a gift from you that was sweet and simple and didn't cost anything extra. No conniving. Nothing on a grand scale. Not a gift meant to top all gifts, just a gift that showed you thought of me."

"I think of you all the time."

She squinted at him. "Then it should be easy." Sometimes her voice slipped backwards in time and sounded fragile and hopeful and childlike. The same as when he would put her to bed when she was small, and she would tease him for sitting on her legs, again. He would slide over, pretending it had been an accident and not part of their game. He would say he loved her very much, and she would say she loved him very, very much, and he would reply with more very's, and she would reply with more, until one of them would say, "I love you with *all* the very's!" and they would laugh.

"I really have to go now. Call next time, okay?" Marta still looked sad for him as she shut the door. He stood there, with Hilda, not knowing what to do with her now, and he could tell his daughter lingered on the opposite side of the door too, because he didn't hear her footsteps moving away.

On the way back down the stairs, Hilda seemed to want to tussle with him. Her legs whacked the banisters. Her hands got stuck between railings. Her head bumped his head. He started to take her painted smirk personally.

Just beyond the base of the stairs, Otto stumbled. He went from looking at the white cement walkway beneath him to staring at the cloudy sky above. Hilda landed flat on top of him, and his head barely missed the concrete, thumping into the damp, mulchy earth beside it. The impact brought tears to his eyes, but Hilda seemed unscathed.

It took effort to right himself and Hilda again. He had hoped to brace himself against her a little to help him stand, but she kept sliding into his way, preventing his feet from gaining purchase or causing his hand to slip across her middle as he tried to push himself up. Finally, he heaved her to the side altogether, then squatted a moment, gaining strength. It wasn't so easy for him to stand from this position at his age.

A row of dumpsters lined the sidewalk where the parking lot began. He considered hoisting Hilda in there, but the prospect of Marta bringing her own trash down later and seeing Hilda's legs poking up stopped him.

Clouds leftover from the day now banked along the horizon. Fallen redbud petals floated in puddles, browning at the edges and turning mucky. Other tenants noticed Otto as he limped and dragged Hilda down the sidewalk. Now their expressions seemed jeering and fraught. Maybe everyone saw in Hilda what Marta had. Saw in him what Marta had.

Eventually he made it back to his car and, once again, slid into the passenger seat, lugging Hilda in on top of him. He sat there, his hands wrapped around her cold plastic middle.

He might have cried if he hadn't minded how that would look to people passing by outside the car. So he wriggled out from under Hilda again and shut her door with an air of gallantry.

Before he put the car into gear, he fluffed his hair one more time. Another few slivers of bark shivered into his lap. He turned to Hilda. "Well, liebling, nothing ever goes as planned, does it?"

The permanent smirk on her face seemed to put him in his place. He didn't talk to her for the rest of the ride home. When he pulled into his building's parking garage, he left her behind, alone. He canceled dinner plans with friends and ate toast with melted cheese by himself in his empty penthouse apartment.

As his first step to getting ready for bed, Otto emptied his blazer pockets. His car keys. Yet another errant chunk of mulch. And the mostly empty package of Utz sour cream and onion. He examined the bag for a moment. This was a simple thing that he liked. No conniving required. No extra cash.

Imagine Utz sour cream and onion and two or three other little Jiffy-J items, wrapped in nothing more than a Jiffy-J red plastic bag. He would take Marta to eat at the taco truck that parked in the lot outside his building during the work week lunch rush. They would sit by the train tracks, because Otto had always loved train tracks. The faint smell of creosote. The tracks creeping out of view into infinity. The whole rest of the world lying just beyond.

He would share a handful of simple things he really liked and she would stare at him, uncomprehending, because what else could she do? Who would want to share such basic, boring things?

Before bed, he texted Marta. "Doing like you asked and planning instead of dropping by. Would love to take you to lunch tomorrow." In person, a barely tolerant sigh would likely accompany her answer, but Marta's response only said, "Should work. Finishing paper now." He asked her to meet him outside his building so they could walk together.

Really, Utz sour cream and onion was a much funnier gift than Hilda ever could have been.

———

His giddiness about his task the next morning made Otto forget Hilda altogether until he climbed back into his car and the sight of her peering at him from the passenger seat startled him. "Hilda," he said. "What am I going to do with you?"

The way Otto saw it, his mission was simple. Go back to the Jiffy-J, get another bag of the Utz chips, and find two or three other things that bore some connection to his daughter. At least when Marta seemed disappointed by an offering of cheap oddities from the convenience store, her reaction wouldn't hurt him. It would make sense.

Otto fired the ignition and cast another glance at Hilda before backing out. "She should have you liked you, liebling."

It was a sunny day, yesterday's drizzle forgotten but for a few small puddles and patches of mud. Flowers bloomed cheerfully in medians. The grass and all the new leaves were greener from the rain the day before. In the parking lot of the Jiffy-J, Hilda shone as red as tulips from the front seat.

The clerk inside was the same one from the day before, and he winced when he recognized Otto. He craned a look at the car parked out front and rushed from behind the counter with waving hands. "No, no, no, sir!"

"What is it?" Otto asked, looking all around himself for a cause for such concern.

"I'm sorry," the clerk said, peeking back toward Otto's car again, "but a deal's a deal. I can't take that thing back."

"No, of course not."

"As long as we're clear," the clerk said. "I almost lost my job over that thing."

Otto glanced backwards toward his car now too. "Over Hilda?" But of course the clerk would have no clue who Hilda was, and his face showed his confusion. "The M&M, I mean. You almost lost your job because of that?"

"Yes, sir. Never seen my boss so mad. Even after I handed over all the money."

"Was it not enough?" Marta's remarks from her doorway yesterday came back to Otto. Something about an unsuspecting kid. He reached for his pocket, with the thought of offering more, but the clerk's eyes bugged and his hands shot out to stop him.

"There's cameras everywhere in here, man. I can't just take your money. Not again. And I can't sell stuff that's not mine. Just, if you don't mind, please don't hang around for long with that thing out there, okay?"

"Certainly," Otto said. The clerk nodded, only half-satisfied, and headed back to his station behind the counter. He fiddled with a display of caffeine tablets, then checked outside again, looking harried.

The counter, and the whole store for that matter, seemed a riot of bright yellows, blues, and reds. Plastic packaging and glossy magazine covers glared from every aisle and from the ends of every aisle and from stands along the counter too. The colors banded together and seemed to collect into a raucous noise that began to bother Otto. He wanted to get out of there as quickly as the clerk wanted him gone.

The Utz sour cream and onion were, of course, where they always were, and Otto eased a package from its display clip. Now for the other two other gifts.

On one aisle, he found motor oil and tampons and cans of soup whose labels sported gruesome pictures of what the soup inside was supposed to look like. To Otto, it all looked like dog food. In fact, to the right of the soup were cans and bags of dog food, and diapers. He switched aisles.

So much American candy, which he had never liked, but it was a small store, and he was running out of aisles. He had a challenge to satisfy, and a point to prove. The point that the kind of gifts Marta was asking for were meaningless. The right selection of simple little tokens might convince her that grand gestures weren't so bad after all.

No to the fireball candies and to the myriad American milk chocolates that had almost no flavor. No to the vast array of bubble gum. He was about to give up altogether when something from a low shelf sparked his fancy at last. A familiar paper roll of candies.

Necco wafers, pale little disks he remembered from Marta's childhood. Their sugar powdered your fingers, and they cracked like chalk, with a mere figment of flavor faked to correspond to each of the pastel colors. His mouth watered at the memory, not in anticipation but in a reflexive rush of cleansing. When given the chance, though, it was the candy Marta had always asked for. So he bent and retrieved a roll. It fit in his hand in a snug, satisfying way.

The clerk cleared his throat and gave Otto a pleading smile from behind the counter. Imagine a job so tenuous that a plastic creature could threaten it. Otto hadn't considered such a possibility in all his life. He nodded in the clerk's direction, a cue that he would hurry, but he needed one more item.

Accessories with no seeming relation to one another jammed a stand at the end of the candy aisle. Magnets. Packs of playing cards. Lighters with decorated cases. Key chain fobs emblazoned with various touristy images: tiny Blue Ridge Mountains in metallic relief, several variations on Monticello, a Thomas Jefferson bust that doubled as a bottle opener. People would buy anything.

Then again, he had bought Hilda.

From the back of a rack of "Virginia Is For Lovers" keychains, something bright and green flashed in the fluorescent lights. Otto brushed the other fobs out of the way until he held the last one between two fingers. It was a tiny metal frog, lime green with four darker green dots and a streak of yellow for its belly. It sheltered under a red and white toadstool and immediately called to mind those ill-fated pollywogs.

The death of those tadpoles had proved something to Marta about the world—its ruthlessness, her father's powerlessness over it, and, worse than that, her father's ignorance and the harm it could cause.

That silly little frog surprised a knot into Otto's throat, as if it could fulfill the promise the pollywogs, and so many of his own subsequent failures, had broken. With his free hand, he dug his lavender-scented handkerchief out of his blazer's breast pocket and touched its edge to the corners of his eyes. Then he re-pocketed it and worked the keychain free from its display prong.

The clerk seemed happy to see Otto stride up to the counter, finally, with his three items in hand. The total came to a pitifully small sum and the booty hardly filled the bright red Jiffy-J bag, which swung from Otto's hand on his way to his car. Again, before he backed away, he waved to the clerk, who, visibly relieved now, waved in return.

———

Back in his parking garage once more, Otto debated Hilda's fate. "It's been a lovely go of it," he told her, "but ultimately it hasn't worked out." Her smirk was starting to unnerve him, and the Christmas hat wasn't funny anymore. He wanted to blame her for disappointing his daughter yesterday, and for his growing unease about seeing her again today, and there was no one to contradict him.

The parking spaces were not large. Removing Hilda without whacking his car door against the Porsche beside it proved difficult, and Otto wasn't entirely certain the doors hadn't bumped one another. In the dimness, he couldn't tell for sure if there was a smudge of metallic gray in the center of the cobalt blue sports car's door.

Hilda struggled, but not as much as she had coming down Marta's stairs. Otto liked to think she had learned something in their two days together. He lugged her over to the dumpsters. The scraping of her plastic boots along the pavement echoed in the tight space of the garage. It was one of those irritating sounds that prickled Otto's spine.

If he had any skill at physics, he was sure he could deduce the best way to lever Hilda up and into the garbage. Not only did Otto lack such skill, he also lacked time. He had a few emails to return and a couple of grooming tasks to complete before meeting his daughter for lunch, so he stood with Hilda beside the dumpster to think.

She leaned into him so that someone from behind might mistake her for some kind of companion. At this thought, Otto shot a conspiratorial glance Hilda's way, and her painted sneer seemed to share his joke again.

Throwing her away seemed cruel now. Why not just leave her here? Set her up beside the dumpster like people did with furniture they meant to give away. Marta hadn't wanted her, but maybe someone else would. Otto bobbled her to and fro until her white boots found their balance. "There's hope for you yet, Hilda," Otto said, and he touched a fist gently to her cheek.

———

Sleek, modern, and new, Otto's apartment building sat on Water Street, sandwiched between the parallel lines of the downtown pedestrian mall and the railroad tracks. His penthouse view opened onto tiers of city rooftops and undulations of the nearest Blue Ridge foothills. But the building spilled you onto cramped backstreets and acres of public parking lots and garages. He emerged into this backdrop to meet his daughter.

His invitation only promised lunch. He hadn't mentioned the gifts, tucked in his blazer pocket in their Jiffy-J bag, and he hadn't warned her that their food destination would be one of the curbside trucks parked across from the Water Street garage.

Marta arrived, right on time, in a cotton dress he hadn't seen before, a faded brick shade that buttoned up the front. She left her hair down today, and it billowed in the soft breeze. It was wispy and light, looking far more carefree than she usually seemed. She had left her reading glasses at home, giving a clear view of her eyes.

"I'm glad you could make it, Marta," he said.

"Planning ahead helps." Her careful tone reminded him how often she asked him to make this kind of plan and how rarely he did. Maybe he should have tried, at least once, to do as she asked before making this strange joke of it.

"I have to warn you, right from the start, that I'm planning some surprises," he said. "Including gifts."

A sense of dread flashed on her face.

"Little surprises," Otto said. "I promise."

Marta breathed out. "Good." But he could tell she didn't know if she could trust him. Her stiffness chastened him, and a twinge of worry pinched his stomach.

"I want to take you to my favorite lunch spot," Otto said.

"Am I dressed okay?" she asked, turning toward him for appraisal. The dress was nice enough, simple, slightly tailored, unwrinkled, and tidy. Obviously, she thought he meant to take her to one of his usual favorite upscale restaurants or clubs and was simply checking to be sure she met the potential dress code, but still it struck him what a reflex it was for her to ask him to judge her worthy or not. So he didn't question the dress's provenance the way he often did. Today he tried to duck the feeling that her preference for Goodwill was one more way for her to control the distance between them.

"You look lovely," he said instead. Her surprise at his compliment hit him like a slap.

The taco truck was inelegant, painted a shade of turquoise that reminded Otto of beach towels. They walked toward it, which was the same direction as the downtown mall and a host of other possible restaurant destinations, so Marta didn't know where they were going until Otto pointed to the truck and announced, "My favorite food in town."

In fact, the tacos here tasted better to him than any meal at his club's five-star restaurant. But there was no enchanting view, no sense of occasion.

"Tell me what's good," Marta said, squinting at the menu painted on the side of the truck. She seemed at ease out here, relieved, with the wind tossing her hair. Two other people ahead of them talked about a music festival slated for the weekend. Otto pointed out his favorite taco combinations, and when it was time for them to order, she chose the ones he mentioned.

"I was thinking we could sit by the train tracks to eat," Otto said. He loved to be near the tracks but couldn't imagine why anyone else would. The backs of buildings that lined them looked industrial and dirty. The area around them was graveled and weedy.

Marta wiped a strand of hair away from her face as they walked from the truck to the tracks. "Train tracks always seem to be leading somewhere," she said. "No matter what you feel like looking at them, like if you're having a bad day or feeling stuck about something, they take you away with them."

Otto laughed with recognition. "Yes!" he said. "I feel exactly the same."

They lowered themselves onto a discarded railroad tie that sat twenty or so feet beyond the tracks, weeds high behind them. They peeled back the tacos' waxy wrappers and crouched forward to let them drip onto the ground. Once, when some meaty juice dribbled down Marta's chin, Otto reached out and dabbed it away with his own napkin, and she let him.

Sitting on the railroad tie, they were nearer to each other than when they usually dined together. Otto liked the closeness. He spent a lot of time alone, and the handful of people he spent time with were mostly business colleagues. Even when they were his friends, they weren't people he loved. It was different to sit with someone he loved.

"I like this," Marta said. Her hand cupped the crumpled wrapper of her finished taco.

"The food?" Otto said.

"No," she said. "I mean, yes, I also like the food, but this. Sitting here with you. We've never done something like this before."

Otto thought a moment what other things like this there may be, because now he wanted to do more of them. Then a train rattled in the distance. A memory flashed from his own childhood, holding his father's hand to watch a train clatter through an Alpine village they were visiting for summer vacation. The feel of his father's hand, closing around his, a tightness that meant love and safety. The train that meant adventure and life rolling on and on.

It was a freight train, first clacking one slow car at a time, gaining speed as the engine passed the city limits. They had to stand up and step back to let it rumble past. Their taco wrappers fluttered in the train's wind. Marta counted up to seventy-five cars before she gave up.

"Lunch beside the train tracks, complete with train," Marta said after the last car shuttled past. "That was really fun."

She was saying goodbye, he realized, preparing to walk back to her car and to whatever schoolwork she needed to get back to. "But wait," he said. "I still have presents."

He couldn't remember the last time they had shared time so happily together, unless it was all the way back to those bedtimes with all the very's. The presents were the only pretense he had to stretch this moment, even though now he expected they would ruin everything, these things he had bought in jest to prove her wrong about what she said she wanted from him.

A car crossed the tracks beside them. Gravel crackled under the tires.

"They're nothing," he said. He scooped the worthless red plastic Jiffy-J bag from his pocket and traded it for her spent taco wrappers, unsure which handful was more fit for the garbage. "I tried to take your advice. They're just some things I liked." He spoke quickly, nervous and ashamed now.

She accepted the bag with a curious smile. The first thing she lifted out was the biggest item, the chips.

"Another favorite," Otto said, "like the tacos. They're cheap, of course. Not worth a thing, but I like them."

She ripped the bag open, tasted one, and offered him a couple. "They really do taste good, don't they?"

It hadn't occurred to him that she might like them.

Next she pulled out the Neccos. "One of *my* favorites this time," she said. "Sweet of you to remember."

He couldn't tell if she was just being polite, but she seemed touched. By a cheap roll of candy.

Last out of the bag was the key chain, smaller than Otto remembered. She placed it in her palm and held it up for a good look. "It's cute."

"I don't know if you even remember what it reminded me of," he said, "that summer I brought you the jar of pollywogs?"

She nodded, still assessing the little frog. "The ones that died, you mean?"

"You were so sad," he said. "As if you'd just learned about all the unfairness of the world."

"And this little guy is meant to cancel that out?"

"Maybe just a little?" He touched the frog in her palm and connected his gaze with hers. Why were her eyes always so sad and serious?

She pulled her keys out of her purse, and he was sure she was about to rush off and leave him there. Instead, she threaded her keys onto the new fob. "It's a nice idea, Dad," she said, and she kissed his cheek.

She hadn't done that in a long time, so he laid his hand on top of the kiss as if he could hold it there.

"But you know gifts don't work that way, right? They don't erase the past."

"Did I do something wrong?" Otto asked.

He could see she was weighing the question in her mind. "No, not this time." She might have had more to say, but she added nothing beyond thanking him for lunch and saying goodbye.

He smiled at her and waved as she walked away. Relief that she had loved his pointless little gifts, the tacos, the train tracks, had loved him, even, for a moment or two, vied against a deeper unease. Because he had no idea how to do that again. How to make her feel the way she wanted to feel when she was with him.

Afterward, Otto slipped back into his apartment building through its parking garage. He had the urge to talk to Hilda. "Liebling," he might say, "you won't believe what just happened." And he would spin the tale of buying all the items from the Jiffy-J. He would exaggerate their worthlessness and the garish colors of the store. He would try to describe Marta's simple appreciation for his ridiculous efforts. "And the joke's really on me, Hilda, isn't it?" he might say. "I tricked myself into being sincere." Hilda's smirk would share the joke.

After the sunshine, the darkness inside blinded him. He eased his way slowly along the concrete wall and waited for his eyes to adjust to the dim garage lighting.

First he heard giggling, then, closer, he saw a mother and her little daughter standing in front of Hilda.

"How are you today?" the little girl asked.

The mother answered in a funny voice, "Not so bad, yourself?"

The girl laughed, like hundreds of tiny bells ringing, and Otto knew Hilda had nothing left to say to him.

He kept out of view and continued along the wall all the way to the elevators. When he came back down later, Hilda was gone.

Regular English

Most room maids stay one season, two tops. Eight years makes me some kind of pro. That's why my nametag says Mavis Bouchard: Room Attendant *Manager*, being at the Mountaintop Inn so long and doing what I'm told, both. So I do what I'm told the day Craig Ladney shows me little Miss Jenny Parker and tells me to train her, even though you can tell looking at her she won't last—homecoming-queen pretty, dirty blond hair falling in kinks around her face. You can feel the prissy glowing off her right along with the shine on her teeth.

"Rule number one is do whatever Craig Ladney says. He's the boss," I tell Jenny. "Rule number two—take whatever comes your way and clean it the fuck up. And rule number three—blend with the wall paint. Far as these guests go, we're not even here."

She nods like she gets it, like she'd do anything you said, but that whole first while together, I'm waiting for the prissy to take over the girl.

Think how long it'll take a girl like her to learn how to scrub a toilet, change a bed, and leave a room fresh in no time flat. Her with half-moons on her fingertips, starshine coming out her eyes. Then think how long it'll take us to find the next one when she gives up and leaves. I'll be cleaning twice my normal rooms and dragging my Rosalee home late to bedtime for months to come.

First stop's the utility room off the 100s hallway. The dryers stand at the back, big enough to swallow you up. We got maid dresses in the closet to fit about any size girl cause of all the coming and going. They're polycotton and soot gray with a round white collar. Hanging there in a row they look dull as socks until Jenny walks out wearing one. Might just as well be a ball gown on her, the way it snugs up against every rise and fall of her body.

In the bins by the dryers, we got a day's worth of clean towels to fold, plus toiletry items on the shelves to restock the maid carts, so we get to work. Jenny Parker folds washcloths into perfect squares straight off. She squirts out words like "cute," right after she pulls on that maid dress, then again when she gets her hands on those little wrapped-up soaps and tiny shampoos.

"Cute?" I spit out the word. Every damn thing about Jenny is cute, from the perky uptilt of her nose to her bright blinky eyes. What does she know about a job like this? About cleaning up messes bad enough to show up in your nightmares?

"Ain't nothing cute about this job," I tell her. "You wait and see."

First day I keep her at the laundry doing inventory, a job I been putting off for weeks. Something about setting Jenny Parker up to count towels and bedsheets the day through makes me chuckle all the way down the hall with the cleaning cart, even if I got to carry a double load until her training's done. I been on my own with a double load all week as it is, ever since Manuela called from New Jersey saying she moved.

———

At the end of that first day, I pick up Rosalee from my mama's house, rush her home, bustle through her bath just so we get a few minutes together, me pulling my feet up alongside hers on her bed for reading time. Rosalee's partial to princesses. Up to me, I'd skip them altogether unless every last one could be like Cinderella. You got to respect a girl who knows how to get dirty, don't shrivel up when the work gets hard. Not too many like her, though, so I make up extra characters.

"You hear tell about the princess's best friend, Tallulah?" I ask Rosalee. "She went on up to the community college and got her a LPN license."

"She did?"

I love the way her voice sounds when she's sleepy, so small and far away, the way the knob of her head rests warm against my arm.

"Yeah. She had to study real hard and stay in school, but now she's the hero of the whole hospital."

"Does she get to wear party dresses?"

That's what Rosalee wants to know. Party dresses.

"A working girl gets to wear a uniform," I tell her.

"I want me some party dresses," she says, half-asleep already, so sure she would've been wearing a gold crown on her head and ordering people around all day long, eating fancy cakes taller than her mama if she'd lived back in them olden days. I don't tell her how there's always been more folks taking orders than giving them. Wiping up toilet seats. Chucking out garbage. She'll figure that out soon enough.

Next day Jenny shows up looking like a fashion magazine in her little gray dress. I tell her she's ready to work some rooms with me. I'm hoping for the worst kinds of messes just to see what she'll do.

Lucky for her, first room we come to ain't so bad. Husband and wife. You can tell they got their own system to live by from how they got their little stacks of things just so. His pocketful of change and notes to himself on the one side of the bed. Her lip balm and book to read plus half a wadded up tissue on the other.

Looks like they come up for a day or two of hiking the Appalachian Trail. All you got to do to get to the AT from here is walk along the highway about half a minute, cross over, and disappear into the woods at the white blaze. I like to picture that myself sometimes, wandering up there after work one day, slipping into the trees, walking till my legs give out, then laying back on the dirt and rocks and staring up into a wide-open night sky, black but for the stars peeping back at me. Nothing but me and my thoughts for a zillion miles.

But I got places to be.

The husband and wife are staying one more night, so I show Jenny how to make the bed, smooth everything so it looks like a machine could've done it, tricks for how to get the spread to tuck around the pillows. "It's all in the wrist," I tell her. She shadows my every move, tries them out for herself.

Next room ain't too bad neither. He's a one-nighter, so Jenny gets practice ripping sheets off a bed before we come upon the mess in the bathroom. Now we're talking. Man must've shaved his beard off into the sink. Looks like a head coming up out of the drain.

"We get a lot like him," I say. "Maybe hiking the whole AT, stopping here cause it's nearabout halfway. This motel might be the first time he's seen the inside of a room since Georgia or Maine. Look out, too. Sometimes what you find in trash cans in these kinda rooms don't sit well with the stomach."

Jenny wrinkles up her nose, a mixture of grossed-out and curious. "Like what?"

"Bandages from blisters five states old, pairs of shoes worn through the soles, stinking like an army of men died in there."

Jenny keeps her nose pinched, but she swabs every last bit of hair out of that sink.

Next day brings the exact kind of test I been waiting for. Drunken frat boys in this room, looking for a wild night some ways out of town. "You take the interstate one hour either direction, you're at one big old college or another," I tell her. "Never know what you're gonna find in one of their rooms."

Jenny hovers at the door. I knew this kind of room'd be rough on her, and I feel almost sorry. But I can't have her calling on me whenever she comes across a mess like this one. So I square my hand against her back and shove her forward.

"Frat boys try just about anything drunk," I tell her. "Hike after sunset. Swim in the pool. Run naked up the highway. Sometimes they get too fucked up, think they're in the bathroom when they're standing by the bed. This was some drunken frat boys in here for sure."

Trash cans full of puke. "At least they made it into the can," is what I say. I peel out the plastic liners, spray some disinfectant. Jenny looks swoony. But she goes over to the bed, smart enough already to snoop around the covers for surprises before she pulls them off. She makes a tidy pile, then she's back at my elbow, watching and helping.

The bathroom's another room full of sick. Plus, empties— cans and bottles—fill the bathtub. "Jesus," Jenny says. "We oughta have Hazmat suits."

Imagine her and me in a couple of them bright orange jumpsuits straight off one of them cop shows. We'd look almost alike. Not like in these clingy maid dresses, showing my fat shoulders and big broad ass as compared to Jenny's plum-perfect breasts and firm little tush.

Break time, we prop up our feet. Jenny grabs a snack and a book from her purse. Some kind of nut and seed combo you might toss out for birds in winter. And I can't even read the title of her book. "Eating bird food and reading 'Tangerine?'" I say. It's not the right word, but it's the closest I can get.

She smiles at me, showing those too-white teeth. She says a word in French that don't sound a thing like tangerine, and she tells the name of the guy who wrote it, a name that looks a whole nother way from how it sounds too.

"It's French for the stranger," Jenny says. "It's about a murder. Mostly about feeling like an outsider, though."

"What's the title in French for?"

"The whole book's in French."

The way she says it, you'd think it's normal as pie to sit in the break room of the Mountaintop Inn reading a book in French. I shake my head, pick up a *People* magazine from the floor, and thumb through a whole bunch of trash about rich famous people. This one's back in rehab, that one's got a baby bump, all these other ones with their plastic surgery. But I'd never be sitting in a room with any of them.

"What you reading that book for?" I ask.

"I like it. I'm going to major in French literature in college. That's what I'm saving up for."

Saving up for. Like you could get to college from here. For most folks, this is the place you go when there's no place better to choose from, but here she is, ready to waste my time and hers, learning this job just long enough to turn right around and leave it.

"So, what? You starting college in the fall?"

"I did my first year already," she says. She rolls a pinch of bird food between her fingers.

What did Craig Ladney expect when she walked in, job application swinging from her baby-soft little hand? Did he even ask if she planned to stick around? Probably didn't think past looking at her. And looking at her's all he has to do. I'm the one stuck for months training her then retraining whoever comes next. I'll be sending postcards to Rosalee before long with all my extra hours. "So when do you head back?"

"I don't." Jenny's lips close up around her shiny teeth. "I guess you could say the money ran out."

I hike myself upright in my chair. "Ran out?" I can't picture Jenny Parker racing up to the utilities office before the stroke of five to keep her heat on for the weekend or putting back the Nilla wafers and baby carrots cause the grocery bill ran too high. "How's that?"

"I was supposed to do an internship this summer."

"*This* summer?" All I know about internships is they make better jobs than this one. "And you wound up here?"

"My daddy set it up for me with some friend of his. When I didn't take it, he said I could just make my own money from now on."

"Hard to argue with a man who wants his daughter to work for a living."

Jenny says, "Huh." Then she looks off into the dusty back corner of the break room and keeps talking. "I show up for my interview, right? Guy says my daddy didn't tell him how pretty I was." Jenny closes her eyes and hunches her body in toward itself like she's one big fist getting ready to strike. "He had some pretty specific ideas about what I could do for him in that internship."

Jenny keeps her lightning-bug green eyes fixed on the corner. I tug at the back of my shoe, trying to give relief to a blister there, and what do I see but the dainty little black flats on Jenny's perfect little princess feet? Me with ugly-ass fat-soled nurse shoes and blisters. "You couldn't just talk him down?"

"Talk him down?" Like she was the only girl ever had some asshole get the wrong idea about her.

"Yeah, talk him down. Offer less than he's asking but keep the damn job. Instead of spending the summer folding towels and scooping puke when you could've been someplace better."

"Better? I can work in peace here. Blend with the wall paint, like you said."

"Give me your life for one day," I say, winding up.

"Come on, Mavis. No way you'd stand for shit like that."

"Who knows what I'd stand for?"

"If it was your daughter in place of me?"

"Rosalee don't get nothing handed to her so easy as that. Wouldn't catch her turning down so gold a goose."

Jenny shakes her head at me. "Well, I kicked the bastard in the balls and walked out."

Picture Jenny with her tiny shoulders squared. Some dumpy ass-wipe of a man with a waddle shaking under his chin, talking dirty to her. Then the look on his saggy face when her foot comes swinging into his unsuspecting prostate.

Jenny zips her little baggie of seeds, crams her book in her purse, and slams her feet back on the ground. "I don't believe you would've done any different."

She walks off before I can say anything back. And I hate that she's right. Put me in a room with some man that talked that kinda trash to me or my girl? Ain't but one of us coming out fit to reproduce, I promise you that.

———

Maybe a week goes by, and Craig Ladney says it's time to open up the pool for the season. Somebody's already been to fix up the chemicals, so when me and Jenny pull the latch on the gate and go out there, the water shimmers up at us all blue and green. It's the first day open, so there's no sopping wet towels growing mildew in a pile, no backup of sticky, crushed beer and soda cans crawling with bugs. Just spent magnolia blossoms floating on top of the water and a frog or two stranded in the filter boxes, bloated and gray. Jenny's hands wobble when she fishes them out with the net. She looks greenish around the jawline, and I'm thinking, *Here it comes.* But she hurls them frogs over the fence and moves on.

It don't take as long to train Jenny as I thought. After the second or third week, she don't flinch at even the fiercest messes we get. Another week or so, and we might be in the break room at the same time, but we ain't pushing the cart together no more. She's got her rooms, I got mine. Mind you, Craig Ladney has to sign off before I can give her the full number, so she's only up to half what she should have, but it's better than it was.

Month or so in, Speak-of-the-Devil pokes his head in the break room. Push-broom mustache polka-dotted with potato chip crumbs. Beer belly jiggling out over his belt and tugging at the buttons on his shirt, same gray as the maid dresses. His pits wet with sweat. Jenny's on to yet another one of her French books and sits there reading it and eating her nuts and seeds.

"You done a fine job with the training," Craig says.

To me or Jenny, neither one of us can tell. We both mumble out a thank you. Jenny packs up and walks out the door, scooting around his wide girth in the doorway. He don't much move out of her way and keeps his eyes fastened at her ass.

"That mean you're gonna give Jenny her share of rooms now?" I ask him when she's far enough down the hallway not to hear.

"Don't wanna chase her off," he says, still staring after the spot Jenny's ass disappeared from. "Don't wanna push her too far too soon."

Same man set me up with all my rooms my third day. Followed behind me, testing my work. Once he hung his hand from the open door of one of my rooms. "Finished?" he said with a face like a skunk just went by. He pulled me in and showed me the toilet seat I'd left flipped up. "That look finished to you?"

How was I supposed to know what finished looked like? Rosalee up half the night before, breast milk seeping down the front of my dress. "I ain't never cleaned hotel rooms before, sir," I told him. Hadn't never stayed at no hotel neither, not that he cared.

He huffed himself up, taller than he already was, and said, "Guests'll think somebody done used it if it you leave it flipped up that way."

But for Jenny Parker all he can say is how he don't wanna chase her off. I burn holes in his back with my eyes while he walks away, but you know he can't feel a thing.

For now, Jenny Parker knocks off early every day. I watch her take her shoes off, stroll barefoot around the pool, dip her feet on in there. Sometimes she spreads out on one of them chaise lounges, hands at the back of her head, staring out at the mountain view like a guest. And here's me, finishing my extra share of rooms till late, getting in each night with hardly enough time to switch little Rosalee into her PJs.

So I start following after Jenny, checking up on her work, hoping to find something wrong, give me a good excuse to shake a finger, tell her a thing or two. But I go room to room. No lazy corners on her tucked-in sheets. Always the right number of clean towels, hanging right-angle straight. All her rooms even feel prettier somehow. I don't find nothing wrong. So I leave one of the doors unlocked. See what'll happen.

A little woman with a shrub of gray hair and red glasses clangs up to the front desk later, yammering about the unlocked door. "I was not aware the doors could be anything but locked," I hear the day clerk tell her. Like she ain't never as much as touched one of the doorknobs around here, didn't even know how the locks worked. The old woman fusses a little more. The clerk gives her a $5 coupon for the Waffle House up the road and tells her she's very sorry.

It's a habit I take to, walking into rooms Jenny's finished with. Think of all the bubble baths Mama or my aunt Sadie's giving Rosalee in place of me. The times I'm glad for a thunderstorm in the middle of the night cause it gives me twenty extra minutes with my little girl, never mind she might be bawling for fear of the noise.

Sometimes I leave a door unlocked, a bar of soap in a sink basin. Spill the hotel shampoo in the bathtub. Leave the toilet seat flipped up. It's not like it matters. Real world don't seem to touch folks like Jenny. Never seems to ask nothing of them either. If it did, you know she wouldn't have no clue what to answer.

By now it's full-blown summer. Days up in the 90s. Air so hot all the blue in the sky bleeds out and leaves it just white. Everything smells like sweat and suntan lotion. You can think of the whole wide world of possible messes we got to clean up poolside. Used condoms floating in the water from folks sneaking in and humping under water in the middle of the night. Baby spew and rotten diapers left out in the sun. Raccoons dragging crap from the trash cans hither to yon. And all the while the polycotton maid dresses slicking your whole body with sweat.

In the break room, Jenny talks on and on about her French books. I get used to the sound of her voice. She tells me the stories in English, making their sexy Paris parties and fancy foods I never heard of sound as close and real as grocery line gossip. I start to tell her some stories of my own. Mine are about regular things, in regular English. About Rosalee and how she hops between my aunt's house thirty miles south and my mama's house thirty miles west, how she wakes up in the night sometimes and don't know where she's at, walks into a wall trying to get to the bathroom. I tell her about Rosalee's daddy and how he walked out on us when she was still a baby. She had the colic so bad she could cry five hours straight. Willy'd bury his head in the pillows, then shout out, "What the hell's wrong with that kid, Mavis?" He used to talk like babies was something you got at the Walmart, and if they come out wrong, you could just head back up there and trade them out. I tell her how, when Willy left, I said a little thank you up to God, cause I swear life got easier from there. Rosalee even started crying less.

Maybe I tell all this to Jenny to prove how hard I work or maybe cause I never had nobody to tell before. "You tell a good story, Mavis," Jenny says. "Just like my French ones, with all the right amounts of heartache." She teaches me words too. *Serviette. Savon. Clé.* Makes what we do sound classy.

Still, every day, after she finishes her half-ass share of rooms, she slips off barefoot to the pool, and I slip myself into one of her cleaned-up rooms and slather a sink faucet with lotion or leave a blob of conditioner on a toilet seat. Makes my extra rooms that much easier to bear.

One time I pulled all the hair off the brush in my purse and jammed it in the bottom of my shoe so I could stopper a sink in one of Jenny's rooms later, fill it with water, and float that clump of hair in there. But before I left the room, I peeked backwards. It looked so ugly I had to fish it out. I flushed it down the toilet, drained the water out of the sink, then twirled the toilet paper roll one or two spins and left it dangling instead. Just one imperfect thing.

One clear-sky day, halfway through August, the hot sun's boiling down like hellfire. Except for us cleaning up after everybody, anybody outside is in a bathing suit, half of them in the water. There's mounds of towels squished up into soggy puddles every time we check for them. Styrofoam coffee cups from the lobby self-serve scattered around, forgotten hair bands, candy wrappers. People will make a mess, that's one thing I learned on this job.

A woman in a red bikini's floating her little baby round in circles in the pool. A man sits on the edge with his feet in, baby-talking at them now and then. One or two college girls are frying up their skin in the sun. Some shrimp-faced old lady's tippy toe-ing in at the shallow end. A crow calls out from the trees on the downhill side of the pool patio.

The slope of the mountain cuts across the sky just beyond.
A big rig engine-brakes out on the highway.

Jenny Parker strides up to our usual lookout—the spot
where we can see all around for what needs cleaning next—
and stares out at the mountains the way she likes. My body
aches from all these weeks of extra rooms to clean. Seems
like Craig Ladney's never gonna give Jenny her full share,
and the day ain't getting no longer. My paycheck ain't getting no bigger, salary being the up and the downside of that
Manager on my badge. I get this urge to run up behind Jenny
and just smack her into the water, dunk her under like my
brother used to do to me in Uncle Lester's cow pond. Hold
you down there just long enough to give you a hint of the
end of the world.

But I keep un-wadding sopping towels and setting them
in the dirty cart. Hurling sogged out diapers into the trash.
Fishing crunched up Styrofoam cups from the filter boxes.

The lady in the red bikini sets her baby up on the lip of
the pool to crawl around in her bright pink and orange
bikini with its little matching bonnet. The daddy coo-coos
at her and claps his hands. Then I think he says something
cross to the mama, and the air changes.

I look back to Jenny. She's running. Nothing else makes
noise or moves. It's hot, but iciness spreads up my back.
The baby was crawling, and now it's not crawling anymore.

Jenny jumps into the pool, dives under the water. The
red bikini mama lets out a shriek. The daddy flaps his arms
like he's trying to fly. Everybody else around the pool's all
the sudden sitting up and looking in the same direction,
just staring, stupid, at the glassy water and the ledge of pool
behind it where a baby's supposed to be.

Jenny heaves back out of the pool with the baby, purplish, cradled against her. The daddy jumps in beside the red bikini mama and both thrash through the water as fast as they can go, aiming for Jenny and their baby. "Oh Jesus, oh Jesus," the dad moans. The mama whoops for air like she was the one about to drown. The two of them climb out at Jenny's feet, and the mama grabs that baby, flips her upside down until she coughs and spews water and milky white stuff. Every one of us watches the purple drain off the baby's face, leaving it pale but for the sunburned tip of her nose. All the while Jenny stands there streaming with pool water like all she'd done was the most natural thing, and I want to know, how did she know what to do and I didn't?

First words out of the mama's mouth I mistake for some kind of thanks until the sounds clatter into clarity. "What the hell you think you're doing? You some kinda lifeguard? You could've killed her. You've could've killed my baby!" Water courses down the woman's face and she clutches her baby to her chest like a splayed frog.

I strut over and shove myself up between Jenny and the shouting woman, my face just inches from hers. "You weren't watching your baby, lady. Every single one of us here saw that." I can smell her sour breath. As for Jenny, water puddles at her feet. Her hair flops wet-dog flat at the sides of her head.

The parents hustle themselves and their baby back off to their mound of towels and t-shirts in a ruckus of crying and a few shouts of blaming each other now that I stared them down from blaming Jenny. Then Craig Ladney's voice rumbles in the distance, asking, "Is there a problem here?" and I remember rule number three about blending with the wall paint. Last thing he ever wants is commotion for the guests.

"Let's get you freshened up," I say and whisk Jenny off to the 100s hallway. Her elbow feels bird-like in my hand, and her eye makeup smears down her cheeks.

She lets me tug her all the way to the utility room. Hot as hell in there with that wall of dryers. She peels her dress up off her head, unhooks her bra, slides her drenched underpants to the floor. I try to look the other way, to not see the milky smoothness of her flesh, the purpled rings of her nipples, goose pimples standing up all over. Soggy and makeup streaked, she looks a bit like a corpse drawn from a lake. But she's still beautiful.

I can see every knot of her spine, though, the ridges of her ribs. "You eating okay, Jenny?" I toss her wet things in with the tumble of drying towels and fetch out a few hot ones.

"Doing the best I can," she says. "Budgeting." And she shrugs a bony shoulder.

She lets me wrap her in the warm towels. It's like holding Rosalee after a bath, but for the smell of chlorine in place of baby shampoo. Jenny lets me tamp water from her mossy wet hair. With her hair flat, her eyes seem twice as big, twice as green. She curls into my attention like she needs it.

"You ever tell your daddy what really happened with that man and that internship?"

"Wouldn't change anything." Jenny wipes her blurred makeup with a corner of the towel. "My daddy's not the kind to admit a mistake."

"Not ever?"

"I'm not waiting around to find out," she says. "I'll save up my money here and send myself back to school no matter how many years it takes. What else am I going to do?"

Me? I fucked around, married the first loser who got me pregnant, and landed here.

Jenny's hair dries back into its perfect ringlets and her makeup-less face stares up like a clean slate, and I see that the biggest difference between her and me's not how pretty she is or how many breaks the world'll give her on account of that. It's how my working hard don't push in any direction, just circles the same old things. Toilet bowls, sink drains, pool tiles. It ain't her fault she's so pretty or that she comes from money and knows a whole part of the world I'll only ever see from the outside. It ain't her fault she knows what to do and I don't.

The dress comes out of the dryer almost too hot to touch, but Jenny stretches it over her head without a flinch. We gather up stacks of clean towels from the shelves by the utility room door and tote them back to where we parked our carts. Jenny flicks a wave at me, heading off toward her last row of rooms for the day, and I think how I'll miss her when she's gone.

"*Savon*," I say to myself. I like the feel of the word in my mouth, even if it doesn't belong to me. Then I shove my cart forward and get back to work.

Trespassing

Their mother knocked on the door and leaned inside quick enough to catch Susan swaying to "The Wallflower" playing on her transistor radio. Elyse, lying across her bed and paging through movie magazines, pretended she hadn't been humming along too, which left Susan to take the brunt of their mother's alarm.

"Susan! That song is *dirty!*" Their mother whispered the last word the same way she whispered *Negro*, as if new music was newer in 1955 than it had been in 1930 when she'd started high school, or even in 1951 when Elyse had. She seemed to blame jazz for every temptation Susan faced in high school hallways and in romance novels she snuck from the library and in cloak rooms after dances when she fantasized about Herman Neville swooping in for one last one-two-three waltz step, a dip, then a kiss that melted into her the same as James Dean with Julie Harris on the movie screen.

"It's not dirty just because it has a good beat," Susan said. She stiffened her posture and plopped to a seat on her own bed, resisting the urge to scissor her legs to the rhythm.

Freshman year kicked off a handful of weeks earlier, and their mother had treated Susan's every behavior since as suspect. She might as well have overheard the other freshman girls trading tales of sneaking into university mixers and stealing first kisses from rough-shaven, clumsy young men they never saw again. Fast as a light switch, Susan's years of cotillion memories splintered into a slide reel of stupid moments drinking lemonade from crystal goblets and waltzing and foxtrotting with sweaty-handed preteen boys. Lessons for a world that didn't exist anymore. Susan wondered if Elyse had felt the same way her freshman year.

"It's the words, Suzy," her mother said. "All that rolling about with Henry."

"You're so old-fashioned, Mother," Elyse said, as if she knew all about rolling around with boys and thought very little of it.

"That's what every girl says to her mother, thinking she knows better." Their mother's tone was smug, her face set tight.

Elyse leveled her gaze with their mother's. "I bet you knew better than your mother sometimes."

"Back in the Dark Ages," Susan added, and the sisters snickered together, savoring their fleeting moment of sharing a target.

Defeated, all their mother could say was, "Turn it down, at least," before she pivoted on her heels and left.

Susan tugged at a loosening button on her cardigan and worked up the nerve to ask Elyse a question she was too afraid to voice in front of their mother. "Don't you think she gets squirrelly anytime it's a song by a Black person?"

"You're always on about that."

"About what?"

"Black people and white people. Like a month in high school makes you an expert on how the whole world works." Elyse huffed her magazine closed and rolled over to sit up.

Susan hadn't realized she'd been on about anything, but ever since the start of the school year she'd been noticing things she hadn't noticed before. At the cafeteria over lunch with a group of new girls the first week of school, one of them mentioned that she never used her back door because it was for the help. A drop of bright yellow mustard flashed at the corner of her lips as she spoke. That, and the snooty sound in her voice, made Susan edge away from her, but what she'd said came back to her later. Susan's family used their back door anytime they felt like it, but she hadn't thought about how it was the only door Miss Francine came or went through. Or how Miss Francine tended hers and Elyse's scraped knees and stomachaches and put dinner on their table, but sometimes after she'd left for the day their father nattered about Black people needing to keep their places while he ate the food she'd made him. Before that day with the mustard-lipped girl, Susan hadn't thought much about what he meant when he said things like that, but now she pictured rows of people lined up in order like items on grocery store shelves. An image that made her understand her father even less and summoned a new whirl of questions.

"Don't you feel like parents tell us what's easy rather than what's real about the world? Or do you think they really believe everything they say?"

Elyse moved to the mirror over their dresser. Her hairbrushes and makeup and body powders crowded the surface. At fourteen, Susan was only allowed to wear lipstick. Elyse fluffed a comb through her hair.

"What difference does it make?" Elyse said. "Things are the way they are no matter what people say." Now she smeared rouge onto her cheeks. Gazing into the mirror, she puckered her mouth into an O to better examine the effects.

"I think it matters what people say," Susan said.

"So prove it," Elyse said.

"Prove it how?"

A noisy mist of hairspray intervened. "Do more than talk." More hairspray, and Elyse bounced a hand where her hair belled at her shoulders, checking its shape. "How about this. We'll go downtown together, only I'll head to Timberlake's for ice cream, and you'll run up to Vinegar Hill. Go walk down their street and buy something from their store and bring it back to me."

Two years older and busy with boys and dance committees, Elyse rarely offered to do things with her, so Susan said yes before she could change her mind. When Elyse was satisfied with her reflection, she dragged Susan with her to ask permission to ride the streetcar into town for an ice cream. Every kindness between them seemed to flatter their mother, as if each one certified her success as a parent. When she agreed to let them go, she even gave them extra spending money for the trip.

Outside Timberlake's, Elyse pointed backward toward Vinegar Hill. "Off you go," she said. "Prove how high and mighty you are."

Going to a store she'd never been to hardly seemed high and mighty. It hardly seemed like anything at all. The day was bright and sunny. Mountain ridges shone purple-blue in the distance. The clerk at the Men and Boys' shop stood in his wingtips smoking at the curb, his Brylcreemed hair glistening in the sunshine. Cars hurtled past, streaming snippets of music. "Cherry Blossom Pink and Apple Blossom White." "Unchained Melody."

She felt eyes on her as soon as she approached the intersection to cross into Vinegar Hill. White men her dad's age scolded her with their expressions. One went so far as to grab her upper arm when it came time to cross. "Ain't no street for white girls," he said, his breath foul with chewing tobacco. She shook herself free and kept going. Once she reached the opposite side of the street, hers was the only white face.

Through the open window of someone's house, she could hear the same radio station she listened to playing the next hit. Wash drying on lines waved in sunlit backyards. According to her parents, or the news, or wherever authority came from, the instant she crossed onto this street she was in danger, but she felt more unwanted than threatened. Children playing in front of their houses stopped when she walked by. Adults peered at her from under hat brims, but their expressions remained still as death.

The pavement and sidewalk were rutted and muddy here, unlike the rest of downtown. Watching her step helped Susan dodge the stern glances. When Inge's store came up on her right she greeted the sign with relief. A bell jangled as she opened the door. Inside everything was spotless and orderly. Ranks of newspapers and magazines stood in front of the register. Along the counter, glass jars of colorful penny candy shone like gems. Nearby, apples and oranges gleamed in perfect piles. She could smell the coffee grinder though she couldn't see it.

The man behind the counter looked up when she walked in, obviously not expecting her. He tried to hide his surprise with a polite nod, but his gesture also carried a warning. She felt conspicuous, as if it were plain as words on a sign around her neck that she wouldn't be here if her sister hadn't dared her to come.

Three boys her age crowded through the doorway after her. They'd go to her school if integration happened. The news said it would, but her father said it wouldn't. One of the boys bumped into her, then leapt backward when he saw her, hands up like at a bank robbery. She bowed her head and stepped out of his way, embarrassed beyond what she normally felt around Herman Neville or other boys she knew.

The clerk asked, "How can I help you?" and threw even more attention her way, so she chose hastily, pointing at the jar of jawbreakers, half as big as her fist. She signaled the number with her fingers, then felt foolish for not speaking. "Two please, sir," she said.

Behind her, the boys jostled along the candy aisle. One picked up a Hershey bar, another a roll of Lifesavers, while the other picked up one thing after another, not able to decide. Their near presence flustered her. One angled his cap over his eyes in a jaunty way. Another wore an Argyle knit vest exactly like one of her father's. Her skin was so pale every emotion showed on it, so she was sure they could read her inexperience and awkwardness in her blush. She stared at her feet, checking the neatness of her bobbysocks, and noticed a red clay streak on the white toe box of one of her saddle oxfords. Her mother would have a fit and make her polish it tonight before bedtime. She would ask Susan where she was walking with a clay mudpuddle, and she didn't know what she would tell her.

The clerk popped a tiny paper bag open with a snap of his wrist and lowered two jawbreakers inside. They made satisfying plops as they landed. She would eat one and save the other for her sister. Proof.

Something thudded to the ground in the produce aisle and a woman let out a gasp. "Oh, Mr. Inge, I'm so sorry," she said. She clutched a hand to her chest and they all beheld a cracked cantaloupe, its guts gushing forth onto the floor.

"Excuse me," Mr. Inge said to Susan. "I'll be right back to ring you up."

The last boy had chosen his candy by now and the group fell into line after her while Mr. Inge fished a mop and bucket from a closet and clattered to the mess in the produce aisle. In this extra moment, Susan second-guessed herself. Elyse would expect something more specific than penny candy, so Susan browsed the magazines and selected one she'd never seen before. Behind her, one of the boys took a sharp breath, the way Elyse often did when they were in public together, overreacting to the littlest things, treating her like a child.

The mop sloshed in the bucket of water. She could smell melon from here. She felt more and more conspicuous with each passing moment and had to steady herself with a long deep breath. Soon enough, though, the cantaloupe would be cleared away, the floor sparkling again. Mr. Inge would take her money and give her change, and she would be on her way, back to her own familiar places, where her sister would be waiting for her, sipping a root beer float and flirting with Larry Tucker, the soda jerk she was sweet on.

Another deep breath and she flipped the magazine open to give herself something to do. She could feel more than see the boys behind her backing away, making room. For what she didn't know. If she were braver, she would whip around to face them, ask them what the trouble was and why they cared about what she did. Instead, all the senses of her body brought her back to a time years before when she'd opened the bathroom door too soon and glimpsed her mother wrapping herself in a towel after a bath. She could feel the moisture of the air, the curdle of her belly, and that same sudden urge to shut a door she shouldn't have opened and run away. Instead, she looked down at the magazine in her hands.

Images punched at her from the page. A boy, her exact age. Visiting family in Mississippi. He went into a market. A white woman complained about him. She remembered a fragment from a radio news story that her father had leapt halfway across the kitchen to switch off before it could finish. Letters in the photo captions joggled in and out of sensible words. Emmett Till. His mother wanted everyone to see what they did to her boy.

That's why the boys had backed away from her. They must have seen these pictures already and would have known she hadn't. She smoothed the pages and slid the magazine back into its holder. She wanted it to look as if she hadn't touched it all.

If Mr. Inge hadn't returned at that moment, swiping his hands against his clerk's apron and saying, "Five cents, please," she would have rushed out the door without the bag of candy. But she dug a quarter from her pocket and held it out to him, then waited impossible seconds for her change. Before she slipped outside again, she stole a last backward glance at the boys in line behind her. All their eyes pointed away from her.

On her way back to Timberlake's, she looked at nothing but sidewalk. Everything else blurred and hushed like radio static. At the door of the shop, she hovered, the candies in their little paper sack swaying from her hand. Inside would smell like sugar, and all the kids would be singing along with a song on the radio. When she joined them, Elyse would twirl her stool to face her and make her tell everyone where she'd been. As if she'd visited a carnival. Then she'd laugh at her for picking jawbreakers, something she could have bought right there in Timberlake's.

Susan spun away from the entrance and hurried home, the whole way on foot. She snuck in through the back door and tiptoed up the stairs to her bedroom. Door closed tight behind her, she tucked both candies under her sister's pillow, then lay on her own bed, closed her eyes, and tried not to see Emmett Till's head, broken open like a melon. She squinted her eyes as tightly closed as they would go and tried to picture something else, but nothing else would come.

If Wishes Were Children

Gladys first spots the little girl on the cereal aisle, tugging at a box of Fruity Pebbles. She's tiny, her head hardly higher than Gladys's own kneecap. She wears a misshapen teddy bear t-shirt and two ponytails that look like they were brushed and put into elastics the day before. The woman who must be her mama wears a ragged cotton dress the color of eraser stubble and rolls their cart ahead, seemingly unaware of the girl. Tired strings of hair wilt into the mama's face from a messy bun loosening down the back of her head. A baby wails in the basket seat. The mama's back reminds Gladys of armor.

If she'd been able to have babies, she never would've hardened to them like that. She would've placed that little girl in the basket too, somehow, keeping her close. Would've put her into a clean t-shirt and shorts before heading out to the grocery store, after combing through her fine hair, so gently. Clipping stray wisps from her face with a strawberry-shaped barrette.

The phantom barrette seems to press into her fingers. It's a marvel how the mind tricks you sometimes.

The second time Gladys sees the little girl, she's pulling toys from the shelves of the seasonal aisle. It's summer, so the girl plunks a bright green pail with a white plastic braided handle onto the dusty tile floor. She clangs around inside it with the attached silver shovel. The mama hears her clatter and rounds on her, her face vicious with anger. "You put that back, Joelle, y'hear? You hear me?"

This time, Wendell nudges Gladys's arm. Ever since her hip started bothering her over the winter, he's been running to the market with her. She can lean into the grocery cart for support when she needs it, but not if she also has to reach out and grab things from the shelves. These days, Wendell's the grabber. Her hip feels better in the warm weather, but she likes his company. They have a lot of time now that they're both retired, but not so much money, so they make occasions out of little things.

"Gladys, I believe you're staring," he whispers.

"I am," Gladys says.

"Well, don't."

In the middle of this exchange, the mama shoots a glance straight at Gladys that says, *Keep your distance.* Or, *None of your goddamn business.* Or, *Help me, for Lord's sake, I don't know what I'm doing.* Whatever it says, it wears a path inside Gladys before it scissors back toward the little girl. She scrolls big eyes up toward her mama, reaches for her hand. The mama swats it away. "Put that toy back," she says again. "*Now!*"

The baby in the basket seat amps up its racket. Sweat wets the back of the mama's dress. Her knuckles on the cart handle shine white against the bright red plastic grip.

Gladys imagines the little girl in their own grocery cart. Not in the seat after all, but standing at the back, balancing her feet on the lower rack and gripping the top edge with her little hands. A gleeful look on her face erases the pasty fear. She wears a pink and green madras plaid sleeveless top with matching lime green shorts, and a pink strawberry clip fastens her hair away from her eyes.

"You're not doing that thing again, are you Gladys?"

"What thing?"

"Where you turn somebody's worst moment into a fairy tale for you?"

For us, she wants to correct, but she says nothing.

"It's not your little girl," Wendell says.

"Of course it's not." His voice is soft enough, but he knows full well how much she wanted a little girl. Or a little boy. How much they both did, but they gave up after six miscarriages. They had no choice. The last one kept Gladys in the hospital for three days of procedures that crushed any straggling hope for babies of their own. All that was long enough ago that their babies' babies could've had babies by now. "But that mama looks like she could use an extra hand, and you know she does."

"I know no such thing," Wendell says. "And neither do you."

Gladys puckers her lips to keep from echoing old arguments. Anyone could see what that mama needs if only they'd look. Picture how much easier she'd have it if she was wheeling through the grocery store this Saturday morning with just one cranky baby. Maybe she'd have more energy. She might've had time to change out of her dingy dress this morning, to feed the baby and tend it, and maybe it would be calm then, and full, and there would be enough love to keep them both happy. The imaginary girl on the cart's edge makes a googly face at Gladys, and she puffs her cheeks and blows air through her lips in response, angling away from Wendell so he doesn't notice.

He's more taken with the array of tissues before him anyway. Studying the boxes, he grows more and more puzzled. "What would you go and put lotion into a tissue for?" His look of pure confusion charms Gladys, the way he probes the world, struggling to see what others see, but sometimes, as in the case of lotion on a tissue, not quite making it all the way there.

"For people with bad colds when they're noses get sore." Gladys reaches around him for their usual, an off brand but not all the way to generic. The generic ones are sandpaper rough.

Wendell consults their list for the next item, and Gladys pilots the cart. As soon as they turn the next corner, there's that little girl again. The real one. She's ripped open a bag of cat food and is spilling it out on the floor. Her nearly colorless shorts sag in back from the weight of a full diaper. Kernels of food funnel out and sift over one another, and the girl watches, fascinated. Maybe she hears the rush of noise and thinks of waterfalls, like Gladys does, but maybe she's never seen a waterfall, and that would be a sad shame.

Often Gladys daydreams excursions with the children she never had—hikes in forests with tidily packed snacks zipped into backpacks, twilit rides on Ferris wheels at the fair. For this child, she imagines waiting in line at that teddy bear store in the mall for an attendant to sew their bear's personal heart into place.

This mama doesn't think of waterfalls or any of that other stuff. Her face flushes from pale to purple. Gladys hunches her shoulders up and squinches her ears, bracing for whatever hateful garbage will spew from that plum-colored face, but the mama's words are quiet. Razor sharp, but quiet. The little girl sweeps her eyes away from the spillage, and maybe the waterfall is lost now and she sees it however her mother sees it—a mess, something else that marks her as a bad girl—because her face droops, her whole body flumps to the floor, and she begins to cry.

The woman says, "Might as well eat that crap right off the floor because it's the last food you'll see for a week."

"She can't mean that," Gladys says to Wendell, plucking his wrist. "She can't, can she?"

"Gladys, turn your eyes away. Everybody has bad days." He grasps the far edge of the cart, nearly grazing the imaginary girl's knuckles. Still at the helm, Gladys coaxes them toward the next aisle.

Flanked by freezer doors now, Gladys halts the cart. "You know if she was ours, we wouldn't speak to her that way."

"That's what you always say." Wendell checks the list again, trying so hard to move on.

"Because it's true, Wendell, we never would've acted like that."

He layers frozen waffles into the cart. "We would've had as many bad days as anyone."

She used to think he said things like this to sneak his way out of grieving, as if he'd convinced himself that their losses had protected them from a lifelong string of disappointments, that they were lucky somehow, but the truth is simpler than that. Somewhere along the line he made peace with what they couldn't have, and she didn't.

The last time they see the little girl, she's ahead of them in line at checkout. The mama hoists the baby on one hip and unloads the basket one-handed. The baby's screaming pitches to shrill and it batters the mama's shoulders with its fists. The little girl plops onto the gritty floor behind their cart and in front of Gladys.

Gladys has never seen a body so sad in all her life and pictures scooping her into her arms and taking her home with them. They would stop at the Walmart on the way home. The little girl would choose a handful of soft toys, plus a jump rope, a bouncy ball. Gladys would splurge on a week's worth of outfits and pajamas, socks and underwear, and she'd rummage the displays of sheets and bedspreads, seeking patterns of bumblebees and stars. With a few swift trips to the basement, they could clear the guest room, switch the new things into it. Gladys stops short of fleeing to the breakfast aisle for the maple syrup she'd need for imagined breakfasts with the little girl.

The girl slumps her elbows into her knees, her face into her hands, and waits. Or lets time pass, as if she doesn't expect anything on the other side of it anymore. When the mama finishes unloading her basket, there's some reckoning with the cashier—an argument over expired coupons, a shortage of change. The little girl doesn't budge.

Gladys considers sliding a ten-dollar bill into the cashier's hand, secretly, to settle the dispute, but somehow the dispute settles itself. The mama plugs the baby back into the seat and shoves the cart toward the door. The little girl remains on the floor in front of Gladys while the mama disappears beyond the automatic doors into a world of hot black asphalt and sunshine glaring off windshields.

"Wendell, we've got to do something," Gladys says, the girl alone now and near enough to be mistaken as their own for real.

"Give her a minute," Wendell says, meaning the mama.

The cashier starts beeping their items through, the conveyor between them hiding the forgotten child from her view. Wendell speaks with her about the heat and last night's thunderstorm.

Gladys wonders why they're giving that mama a second chance when they never got a first one. Shouldn't they be calling the police instead? They'd arrive at once and sort things right out.

That feeling of certainty appeals to Gladys, but her mind sets to work on what sorting things out might look like. First, the police would separate the little girl from her family. A penalty for leaving her behind. Shunt her into foster care. Much as Gladys imagines herself swooping that child off the floor and into their lives, outfitting a room for her and building card houses or chasing butterflies until dinnertime, she knows no one would choose her and Wendell for this little girl. No matter how many forms she might fill out, no matter how many days of desperate phone calls she might make. Not only because it would take too long to process them into the system but also because Gladys and Wendell are old. It hurts them to bend over. This girl will require a lot of bending over. She needs picking up and hugging and help cleaning the messes she'll make. She needs a warm bath and a good scrub and someone to sit down and play with her on the floor.

The foster people would pick someone else—they'd have to—and maybe it would be one of those foster families you read about in the paper who molest their children or beat them or lock them in closets for ten years until the neighbor, an old woman out walking her purse-sized dog, say, hears a noise that sounds like a child crying through the open window of a house where she thought no children lived, and then the exposés, and the six o'clock news, and a thousand years of therapy couldn't undo all that.

They might find a foster family that you don't read about in the news, the kind who do their best to love the children in their charge, feed them, clothe them, educate them. Maybe when the little girl turns seven, they would buy her a used violin and hire a young lady from the city to come teach her how to play it. And she would especially love playing jigs, and while she played her foster parents would dance around the living room, rattling ceramic figurines on the coffee table, or they'd clap along, and tell her what a good girl she was and how talented and how one day she would go to college. But then one of the foster parents would get sick and they would lose their jobs, one by one, and then their home, and they would bundle together in a homeless shelter the first cold day of winter, grateful to be alive but wondering how they got there, and somebody official, taking names and keeping order, would realize the little girl was in foster care and make some calls and the police would come again and take her away from the parents who had almost felt like real parents and had never once yelled at her or told her to eat cat food off the grocery store floor.

"*Gladys.*" Wendell's voice is sharp. The cashier is lowering their last item into the last bag. Gladys swipes her debit card and her special value shopping card so they can get their discounts, and her head swims a little, wondering what to do in a few seconds when it comes time to push their cart forward. They can't walk away with the child still sitting there, and nothing seems like the right thing to do.

The glass doors of the store whoosh open and the little girl's mama storms inside, the baby fastened at her hip again and still screaming, both their faces bright red. "Joelle! Lord, child, you scared me half to death."

The clerk shuffles to attention. "What's this?"

The rage drains from the mama's face. "It's nothing, it's fine," she stammers.

"Did you leave your child behind?" The mama's anger rises up in the clerk's face now. The baby's sobs lower their pitch and hit a rhythm like a train. "We have policies."

"No, ma'am," Gladys says. "We were watching the little girl for her, weren't we?" She nods at the mama. Up close, with the mama's face washed with fear, Gladys sees the very image of the little girl's face peering out across years. Hard years, Gladys sees now, full of impossible choices and constant worry. Never feeling good enough. It's almost too much for Gladys's heart to hold.

The mama nods back at her. "That's right. This lady was helping me out."

The clerk volleys glances between them, not buying it for a second, but she purses her lips, too tired and probably too underpaid to push any further. "Don't do that again," she says. "Not in my store."

The mama nods again, and the little girl stands and brushes dirt from her twiggy legs, taking her mama's hand. They lumber back toward the entrance, the mama weighted down on one side with the now quiet baby and drooping to the other side for the tiny hand. The doors gap open one more time, then close behind them. Another little girl gone forever.

Girl at the Gas-a-Thon

Story always starts with a girl. This one's fro stood about a quarter inch short. Used to work down at the Gas-a-Thon. Nametag said Taysha. She didn't know me.

It was summer, just like any summer—too hot inside, too hot out. At home, we didn't have AC. Didn't have much of squat since Dad left with nearabout all the furniture two years back. Nothing but a junker couch, some duct taped kitchen chairs, and a half-broken TV. That, and the one fan, chopping up hot air and spitting it around.

Nothing left to do most days but walk on down to the Gas-a-Thon. About a mile from my house, just past the giant plaster dinosaur out Route 340. Little cinderblock building. Smelled like gasoline, and piss from the bathroom in the back. Probably hadn't been cleaned the whole fifteen years I'd been alive.

Mid-July, sun bearing down, felt like my skin was melting off. Dodging the one or two cars whizzing around the curves. Sun baking the back of my neck. Heat rising up at me from the road under my feet. Whole time, I was picturing that girl at the Gas-a-Thon, practicing what to say to her. "Taysha. That's one sweet name."

Could've been because I'm white or maybe because I'm not man enough for her yet. Or because Taysha had her eyes on a bigger prize than our puny nothing of a town. Whatever it was, nothing seemed to stop her giving me the same plain-eyed stare at checkout, like she'd never seen me before, couldn't pick me out of a lineup. Even if I did go there every day, buy ten million slushies just to get another look at her.

Didn't matter how many times I practiced it to myself—"Hey Taysha, maybe you and me could hang later. What time you get off?" Didn't matter how many times I pictured her turning my way, listing some-time-o'clock and sliding me her digits across the greasy countertop. Her perfect bright red fingernails poking the tips of my own fingers. Popping the bubble she seemed to float in and making a little room for me there. Didn't matter, because when I shoved open that glass door—ice cold air hitting me square in the face, wiping out summer from all around me—no words came.

All the signs said "No Loitering" so I had this way of kicking around the store, picking up this, picking up that, on every last aisle, to make me look like a real shopper. Up one aisle, down the next. Razors, diapers, rat traps. Tampons, tissues, toilet paper. Candy, gum, Hostess cupcakes. Up and down. Same damn box of Apple Jacks on that back shelf by the bathroom for probably sixty years. Box not even all the way green by now. Whole time I kept watch on Taysha, looking at her through the security mirror or peeking at her out the sides of my eyes.

Most days, after some long time—but not too long—I'd pick something. Pack of Big Red, maybe, Ho-Hos, red slushie, green slushie, pop it up on the counter. "Hey," I'd say, all I ever could get up enough guts to say.

Pretty Taysha would smile, that kind of smile that comes from the inside, doesn't have a thing to do with the person seeing it. The air around her always seemed clearer, shiny. When she looked down at whatever I was about to buy, I could see half lid, half eye peeping out. Made my throat close up. "Hot enough for you?" she might say.

On my own again outside I'd say to myself all the things I should've said back to her. "Hot? Sun ain't got nothing on you." One day, I was gonna be that smooth.

Today it was just too hot to go back outside. Figured loitering might not count if I hid out in the bathroom. Cool off in there long enough to face the sun again and head on home. Maybe with the extra time I'd finally think up something more to say than "Hey."

Bathroom was hardly big as a closet. Reeked of piss and shit and some kind of godawful cherry-flavored air freshener. Sink'd been dripping so long it left dark brown streaks down to the drain. Shut up in there, I didn't see when the guy came in. But I heard the fast noise he made. Opened the door the thinnest line to peek.

This man was standing at the counter, about my height. Noise must've come from his fists banging the counter. Chains hanging off his pants pocket, black ski hat pulled over his face. No shirt at all over his hairy, moon-white back. Jagged scar up one side of his spine. "Gimme the fucking money," he said.

Taysha's eyes wouldn't blink. Her mouth wagged open.

"The fucking money." Man had something in his hand. "Goddammit!"

Taysha jumped back at the sound of his voice. Her eyelids fluttered. Hardly moved another muscle.

Maybe it was because it was so hot that day and my head hadn't finished clearing up yet or because, finally, I had the perfect thing to say. But I threw that bathroom door open and shot up to the front of the store. "Where the fuck you get off talking to her like that?"

Man rounded toward me, thick black hair crawling up his chest like a thousand centipedes. Thunder coming out his mouth. Words mixing with spit. Bushiest eyebrows I ever saw, hulking over the middle of his face. Me marching straight toward him. Taysha in the background shaking her head. Waving her hands no.

Turns out, it was a gun in his hand. Noise cracked through my head. Something hot and horrible tore into my guts. Taysha screaming.

———

When I woke up, everything was white. Nurse came by. I could tell I was in the hospital from her white dress, funky white shoes. "You're quite the hero," she said. She was forty, maybe fifty. Wide ass, mop of curly yellow hair. Lipstick the fakest color red you could think of.

First thing I said, "Girl okay?"

"Yeah. Shook up, for sure," she said.

"They catch the guy?"

"Yeah, he jacked another store a few hours after the one you were in, up in Boyce. There was a cop out front gassing up. The guy didn't make it very far."

Felt like crap, being a hero. Stitches all up and down my belly. They had to cut out some intestines to fix me up. Outside the window, the sun kept burning. At least in the hospital I was cool, cool, cool.

Eyes shut, always seemed like pretty Taysha was sitting in the chair by my bed. Eyes open, it was only ever the big curly-headed nurse with the too-red lips. Her, or my mom, with a dishwater face, smelling like cigarettes. Half the time, Mom didn't talk but just sat there, soaking up the cold air, like I would've done.

"Andy called," she'd tell me. "Robbie."

"What'd they say?"

"Nothing. Get better."

Then she'd leave.

In my sleep, I was sure Taysha came and sat for hours. Reading or flipping through TV channels. Rubbing the back of her soft, soft hand on my forehead. Saying, "You got some serious balls, mister."

Nurse asked me one time, "Who's Taysha?"

"What?"

"You keep saying her name in your sleep. Must be somebody special."

———————

Day they let me out, couple weeks later, all my stitches itched with sweat. Everything hurt. Car stunk like garbage. Windows jammed shut. Had to be about a hundred fifty degrees in there. Thought I'd die before I got home. Mom dropped me off.

"There's stuff for sandwiches," she said.

Doctor said to stay quiet, keep calm, lie down. Only couch we had, though, had springs busting through the cushions. Sheets on my bed were twisted up and filthy from before I left. Stitches kept me from stretching enough to put clean ones on. Nothing left to do but walk on down to the Gas-a-Thon.

Had to keep my arm tucked up under my t-shirt, against my skin. Doctor rigged it that way, keep me from pulling the stitches too much. Figured I looked like a freak, so I threw a flannel shirt on top. It swung out baggy around me. About boiled me on the walk over there.

Hot enough to burn spit on the pavement. Made me dizzy. Had to keep sitting down on the side of the road, praying the next car wouldn't cut a turn too wide and wipe me out. All I was thinking about was seeing Taysha again.

Gust of cold air hit me at the door like always, filled up my lungs. Felt so good, I closed my eyes for a second. I'd stay a good long time today. Maybe pull up a chair. "You see the hair on that guy?" I might say. "That scar up his spine?"

"Weren't you scared?" she might say.

"Didn't have time to be."

Sit there long enough, maybe it'd be easier to walk home than it'd been to walk here. Legs like noodles. Cotton in my head.

This time, Taysha turned when I walked in. Some kind of flowery soap smell whooshed in on the burst of cold air at the door. Then she looked right past me, went back to fiddling with lottery tickets in the display by the register.

Razors, diapers, rat traps. Up one aisle, down the next. Moving so slow, my feet dragged. It'd be better just to sit down. I spied Taysha up in the security mirror, watching me. She was gonna say, "Hey, that's you, isn't it?" any second. "Hey! Let me buy you a coke, something. Boss won't mind." Any second.

Candy, gum, Ho-Hos. Brain so fuzzy, it was hard to pick. That almost-white box of Apple Jacks—cereal had to be sand by now. She was gonna say, "Pick whatever you want, man. You can sit on the stool I got back here. Stay awhile."

I landed my hand first on a Hostess apple pie, then a pack of mini-donuts, then some cheese nips. Back and forth, but I couldn't pick. Tried a few more laps. Legs so slow, I probably looked a little drunk.

"You can't just hang around," Taysha said. First glimpse of me out of the hospital, that's what she said to me.

I dragged myself halfway up the aisle, toward the counter, about to tell her, "Don't you remember me? I'm the guy got shot for you. Remember?" But halfway there, I could see Taysha's eyes fog up with hate.

"You gotta buy something or get out."

"But don't you…"

"Get out. Just go," she said. Voice like a closed door.

So tired, my eyes stayed shut too long between blinks. Eyes shut, I was in the hospital again, picturing Taysha in the chair beside me. Eyes open, there she was, fingers shaking in the air.

Figured I'd just show her my belly. "It's me," and show her the stitches. Practically had to grab my legs with my hands and physically pull myself the rest of the way to the counter.

Closer I got, the more Taysha's eyes flashed at me. Picked up the huge jar of pickled eggs at the cash register too. Hiked it up on her shoulder about to heave it my way. That's what it came to. About to throw fucking pickles at me.

So I stomped the last couple steps. Adrenaline or something steadied my legs. My arm hanging there, strapped to my chest the way it was, must've looked like something pointing at her. I nodded my head toward the register, and suddenly words came easy. "Gimme the fucking money."

Jar of pickled eggs crashed to the floor. Smell of vinegar rose up all around.

"You gotta be kidding me," she said, half-eye, half-lid peeping at me. Clumsy hands fingering the cash in the register, trying to stack it all up to hand it over. Shivering like a rabbit in the road.

A slideshow of all the summer's slushies whipped through my mind. Her hand on each one, nudging it across this same counter at me. All the times I hustled, trying to catch the gaze out of one half-open eye. To see her seeing me. The real me. Not this dumbass backwater white boy scaring the fuck out of her.

"Hang on," I said. Reached my hand toward hers.

She jumped away. Shot her fists up in fight position. Dollar bills fluttered to the floor.

"That's not what I want." Hard to make my voice loud enough. The room blurred. Had to square my weight against the counter. Wait for my balance to come back. The blood to go back to the right places in my body.

"The fuck you want, then?" Her voice was different. Sharper, harder.

"I just want you to remember me."

"Remember you?" The words sprayed out like spit. "You that crazy-ass kid just about got both our heads blown off. I'm not gonna forget you, no matter how hard I try."

"No," I said. "That's not what happened."

"Rushing out on some guy with a gun like some kinda action movie bullshit. What you think was gonna happen?" Her eyes, clear and fierce.

Took all I had to look her in the face one last good time, then walk out the door without falling over. Pain throbbed in my side. Heat waved up off the asphalt, made it hard to see. Never walked slower. Got as far as the ditch where I'd tossed a summer's worth of slushies I'd never wanted and let myself slouch right down in there.

Big rigs flew past every so often. Blasting wind and dirt in my face.

One day I'm gonna flag one of them down. Hitch me a ride someplace else. Someplace better. Find me another girl, little easier to talk to.

Everything Was the Color Red

It gets easier. That's what someone told Mandy at one of her new support group meetings, so that's what she told herself at times like this. It wasn't easier yet, but one day it would be. She pulled into the horseshoe entry in front of Mills School, parked in the lot beyond it, and leaned over the steering wheel for a minute, hoping to summon some kind of mercy.

Pulled hair, poked eyes, thrown toys. What six-year-old's version of violence spurred the principal's call today? Jordie's tiny reign of terror had waged on despite everything Mandy, the family therapist, and a series of teachers and administrators had done and said to help her stop. Mills was a small, private school, and this was the campus for pre-K through second grade. After all the trouble Jordie had with public school, Mandy had hoped the calmer atmosphere and more personal attention of this smaller school would soften her rage.

Mandy tested out her smile in the rearview mirror, adjusted her bangs over the scar that jutted beyond the part in her hair. A few more months and the doctors said you would hardly notice.

Walking toward the building, she zapped her BMW locked as another mother crisscrossed her path, rushing toward the school entrance, her arms overloaded with double-decker trays of cupcakes. Mandy sped up to open the door for her.

"You're a lifesaver." The woman's hair fell neatly to her shoulders, and a light perfume drifted off her.

"No trouble." Mandy imagined a day when having too many cupcakes could be her worst problem.

———

Pamela didn't want to be late for work again. Dr. Bradshaw's Tuesday dental clinic hours were oddball, starting at eleven a.m. and going until eight at night. As his office assistant, her hours had to match his. She should know how to judge the traffic to get to work on time after a year there, but Tuesday's late-morning rush continued to surprise her.

The bottleneck always happened along Preston Avenue, near where she used to live. You were stopped at one light, watching the next one stare greenly back at you, only to turn red as soon as you were moving again. Idiots had planned these lights.

Instead of keeping straight when the light turned green, Pamela turned left to cut out a couple of stoplights. Going this way could add an extra minute or two, but it felt faster.

After she'd made that first turn, she figured why not a few more? Down Oxford, onto Wellford, then Westwood. Over the past few months, she had found plenty of excuses to make this same detour. Her old house wasn't exactly on her way to work, but it wasn't far out of the way either.

She pulled over across the street from it—the brick bungalow with the boxwoods at the edge of the yard. In the short time Pamela had lived there, she had re-painted the shutters a darker shade of red to accent the brick. Now the paint color was the only thing that proved she had lived there at all. The concrete birdbath standing in the front yard was new. So was the bird feeder.

From her perch in her car across the street, Pamela watched a cardinal couple land on the feeder and a scruffy cat trail its lithe body along the outer edge of the boxwoods, tail twitching. Then the woman who lived there came out, a baby on her hip. She spoke to the cat. She had to balance the baby and squat to scratch its cheeks.

What kind of asshole puts up a bird feeder when they have an outdoor cat?

The woman gathered a bundle of twigs from the ground, brush that must have fallen in the last thunderstorm, and eased herself and the baby back upright. That yard was what Pamela and Ray had liked about the place, how it seemed to mix country and city. They had both grown up without much—Ray on a tumbledown farm in the mountains near the West Virginia line and Pamela in subsidized housing outside Norfolk. They were looking forward to living American dream style in this cute little Charlottesville neighborhood.

The woman in the yard faced the road now. She must have caught sight of Pamela's car idling there. The ancient Honda Civic—dented, blue paint peeling down to the primer—looked like the embodiment of bad intentions. Pamela had been planning to replace it before Ray got deployed. Then she thought she would wait until he came back. But he never did.

Foreclosure. It was legal theft. What made people, like that woman—with all her sunshiny hair tumbling around her face and her fat, wide-eyed baby twisting it in its fists—what made them deserve this house more than Pamela? The apartment she moved to from here was in a noisy building that reeked of other people's cooking and echoed with their arguments. You couldn't relax there.

The woman squinted toward Pamela's car, and the look of composure drained right off her face. She braced her baby more closely to her chest, still clutching the twigs in her other hand. "You know you can't come around here anymore," she called out.

Pamela had only banged at the door a handful of times after the new people had moved in. She kept thinking she had forgotten something. All she wanted was to look around. If they had let her in, she would have been perfectly nice. After the first time, though, when they told her they hadn't found anything of hers, they didn't answer the door anymore. Maybe they thought she would go away if they pretended she wasn't there.

But she *was* there. She would knock harder, shout at them. Sometimes the baby would cry. They always called the police.

"There's a restraining order," the woman said.

Pamela cranked the window down and shouted back, "I'm keeping a hundred feet back."

"It's a hundred *yards*." That was what fear looked like—the way the twigs shook in the woman's hand, the expression on her face.

"Oh," Pamela said, "a hundred *yards*. Oops." She gave a fake-apologetic smile and a quick little wave as she drove away. For a minute, she felt better.

The principal's office was cramped, her desk and the floor beside it crowded with extra tissue boxes, huge bottles of hand sanitizer, and buckets of crayons. The walls were papered in cutout mosaics from the pre-K classrooms, trembly-lined stick-figure drawings of families from the kindergarteners, self-portraits in distorted proportions from first and second graders.

"Thanks for coming, Mandy," Mrs. Marshall said.

Mandy knew the drill. An act of aggression caused expulsion from class for the day and required a meeting between the parent and principal. Repeated acts got the student switched out of the class altogether. Mandy tried to remember if this was Jordie's first offense in her latest classroom.

Knees bunched against the principal's messy desk, Mandy endured a couple of phone call interruptions before Mrs. Marshall's assistant produced her daughter. Jordie loped toward Mandy and stood next to her, her forehead level with her mother's shoulder. She looked about the same as she had this morning—her smooth, dark brown bangs hanging in a slash just above her dormouse eyes, two perky ponytails holding the rest of her hair out of her face. The only change, a familiar dullness that radiated off her now. A tiredness so much bigger than the child.

"When children witness violence firsthand," the family therapist had explained, "it affects the way they relate to people for a long time. Some get nightmares. Some cry when a parent is out of sight. Some wet the bed. Some hit."

It had only happened one time, Mandy had wanted to argue. How could a single incident trigger so many after-effects? That single incident, though, had been as recent as six months ago, and Mandy's mother had to hire a special cleaning company to scrub the blood stains from the kitchen cabinets and floor while Mandy recuperated in the hospital. Beyond that, for years before that day, Mandy's husband had taken out his anger on inanimate objects—breaking dishes, smashing chair backs, kicking television screens to smithereens. Jordie had seen it all.

"Do you know why you're here right now?" Mrs. Marshall asked Jordie.

"Yes, ma'am," she said, "because Mommy's here?"

Mrs. Marshall pressed her lips into a tired smile. "No, Jordie. Remember? Your mommy came because we had to call her."

Mandy understood that nobody wanted to tell her Jordie was a problem child. Not after their private tragedy had blazed across local headlines for months. Not after Mandy's husband had morphed from county supervisor into county inmate. Nobody wanted to look Mandy in the eye and say anything but that they were sorry. Why couldn't they call and ask how she was instead? Offer to take her and Jordie out for supper? Invite Jordie for playdates? What good was saying sorry if everybody disappeared after saying it?

"Now, Jordie, tell your mother why we had to call her today," Mrs. Marshall said. "It's important for you to understand. Tell her what happened on the playground."

"Leah wanted the shovel," Jordie said. She tugged at hair escaping from one of her ponytails, plucked at her cherry-print dress. "I had it first."

"Then what?" Mrs. Marshall prodded.

"She took it."

Of course Mandy had thought of leaving her husband before the day he snapped. What if leaving would have made it worse, though? If staying had made it better? You never believed you were in trouble until something happened. He wasn't that kind of man. You weren't that kind of woman. She pulled her fingers through her bangs, arranging the hair over her scar again. Mandy hadn't known what would happen. She was sorry too.

"And then, Jordie?"

"I pushed her."

"And do you understand that what you did hurt Leah?" Mrs. Marshall said.

Jordie had walked into the kitchen that day just as her father punched Mandy's face. Once, twice, three times. Mandy's head thwacked the corner of the granite countertop on her fall to the floor. Before she lost consciousness, she heard Jordie screaming at him, saw her throwing her little body against her father's legs, thrashing him with her tiny fists until he kicked her away from him, cursing, and stalked out of the kitchen, leaving Jordie breathless and Mandy lying on the kitchen floor, blood pooling at her head. A passing neighbor had heard the screaming and called 9-1-1.

These days, Mandy's neighbors walked by her house, averting their eyes. The woman who made the call didn't even come down Mandy's street anymore. No one wanted to believe a thing like that could happen in such a nice neighborhood.

"It wasn't me that made her bleed," Jordie said, scrunching her nose at Mrs. Marshall. "It was the sandbox. I didn't mean to hurt her."

"Not meaning to hurt someone is good, Jordie." Mrs. Marshall tried to sound encouraging, but this was the same answer Jordie always gave. It didn't seem to stop her from hurting someone else. "But you hurt Leah even though you didn't mean to."

Jordie blamed the sandbox again. Leah's head had landed hard on its wooden edge. There had been a lot of blood. "I didn't hit her *that* hard," she said.

Mandy winced. "Jordie." She couldn't think of anything else to say, but she took Jordie's hand in her own. The way Mrs. Marshall talked, the other children had to be protected from her daughter, but Jordie needed protecting too.

Mrs. Marshall asked her assistant to lead Jordie back out of the room for a few minutes at the end of the meeting so she could talk privately with Mandy. School protocol for head injuries required them to call an ambulance, Mrs. Marshall explained. The paramedics had said the wound was not serious, but, understandably, Leah's parents had insisted Jordie switch out of Leah's class.

"This will put Jordie into the last of our first-grade class-rooms," Mrs. Marshall said. "We have to see evidence of change or we'll have no choice but to ask her to leave the school entirely." She folded her fingers together and gave Mandy a grim look. "I'm so sorry, Mandy."

Mandy collected Jordie from the room where she had been waiting and helped adjust her tiny plaid backpack over her shoulders. As soon as Jordie was situated, her hand tucked into Mandy's again, Mrs. Marshall gave a finish-ing smile and said goodbye. Mandy did her best, but in returning the goodbye, she could look no higher than the center of Mrs. Marshall's nose. She was sick of eye contact, sick of all the ways she was expected to receive so much useless sympathy.

———————

Back out on Preston after Pamela's detour, she was running later than ever. And the traffic had gotten no better. She had five minutes to get to Dr. Bradshaw's office. Last time she was late, he had said, "Are you sure this position is working out for you, Pamela?" A nice way of saying, "Next time, you're fired."

The delivery truck in front of her stopped abruptly, and Pamela had to slam on her brakes. Then the truck wouldn't start again. A stoplight ahead of them flashed from green to yellow and back to red before it shuddered back to life. She'd be late to work because that asshole couldn't drive his own truck.

She hated crappy drivers. Traffic. Running late. She hated Tuesdays too, ever since Ray's shitty email came. "Am fine. Need to talk." The rest came out over the phone, on some nameless day of some nameless week. All about the woman he had trained with from his platoon. How they read each other's thoughts. How a roadside IED exploded in a crowded marketplace on their watch. How no one else would understand them after that anyway.

The truck ahead of Pamela had run fine while the light was red, but it stalled again as soon as it turned green. She blasted her horn. The truck stayed still. She blasted her horn again, held it down and kept it blaring.

Whenever people asked about Ray, Pamela told them he wasn't coming back from Afghanistan. She would look sad and change the subject. Maybe they walked away thinking he was dead. She didn't care.

———

Mandy stole glances at Jordie in the rearview mirror, buckled into her car seat, sipping from her juice box. The breeze from the partly open window beside her pushed at her bangs while she dug one animal cracker after another out of the circus-animal box, looking outside and seeing whatever she saw.

The therapist talked to Jordie about things like breathing exercises and counting to ten for the times she started to feel out of control. Mandy was never sure if she should remind Jordie about these techniques when it was already too late to use them. Waiting at the light to turn from Park onto High Street, all she could think to ask was, "Are you trying, Jordie?"

The turn signal clacked, and the engine rumbled quietly. Mandy wasn't sure Jordie had heard her. The light turned green. Most of the cars ahead of them turned left. Mandy waited, waited, turned right.

"I try," Jordie finally said, her voice as dull as the look on her face. "I try as hard as I can."

———

This time, the truck in front of Pamela stayed stalled, and traffic extended behind them in a long, idling tail. Pamela hadn't even made it to Fourteenth Street yet.

Dr. Bradshaw didn't like her anyway. He was probably waiting for his chance to get rid of her. Why stop at foreclosure? She could go for fucking eviction too.

The truck's engine chugged alive again. Finally. Pamela pressed the gas.

Now a car cut into the lane, right in front of her. Some fancy-ass BMW, glowing in the bright sun. A flash of woman's hair through the window, the same shade of golden brown as the woman in Ray's Facebook pictures. The Beemer braked, then braked some more. Pamela had to slam on her own brakes yet again to keep from ramming into it.

She mashed her palm against the horn. Every asshole on earth was in her way today. Being late would be her fault, though. Everything was always her fault, no matter how hard she tried.

Now the Beemer came to a full stop. In the middle of the fucking road. The driver's hand fanned at Pamela from outside her window, waving for her to drive past. As if her high class car made her Queen for a Day.

Fuck work. The Beemer turned onto Grady Avenue, and Pamela followed.

———

That car had been going faster than Mandy realized, and now it stuck to her bumper, seeming inches away. Flashing your brake lights a couple of times was supposed to get a tailgater to back off, but not this one. Waving her on didn't work either. Neither did turning onto another street. So Mandy veered all the way off the road and into an empty parking spot along Grady. She waved out the window one more time.

What more could that nutball want than to pull past her? Instead, the driver swerved to the roadside right in front of Mandy's car, then stamped one foot after another onto the pavement, slammed her door, headed straight for Mandy, shouting.

Mandy powered her window back up. In the rearview, there sat Jordie, eyes narrowed to points. The woman from the other car kept coming. Mandy had gotten out of her way. What more could she do?

Jordie's window was still open a slice, enough to allow the woman's voice to fill the car. She got louder, closer. There was dark, curly hair, a huge pair of sunglasses, a bright pink flash of fingernails, her red, red face looming into the driver's side window, spittle flying from the edges of her lips.

Many times since that day in her kitchen, Mandy had imagined grabbing the sharpest, biggest knife from the knife block that had been right in front of her. She knew exactly how she would have gripped the handle, how she would have aimed it, how much force she would have used to thrust it up and into his chest. Right now, Mandy could throw her car into drive, jam her foot to the floor. She could plow that woman over if she had to.

———————

Everything Pamela saw was the color red—the road at her feet, the Beemer, the woman, the sky—and all the noises blended into a single noise, like metal screeching. The

Beemer seemed to suck Pamela toward it, and she had to make that woman hear her. "I'm right here, bitch! Look at me! Look at me, asshole!"

It felt good to let all that crap spew out of her. It had been so long since Pamela felt like she'd let anything out at all.

Inside her car, that woman was trying to wave her away again, like Pamela was a fly or a hornet. "I'm not going anywhere!"

Pamela ran at the Beemer, one hand on the door, one on the hood, and lurched her face into the driver's window. "You hear me? Can you hear me in there?"

She pounded as hard as she could.

The pounding rocked the car.

"Mommy?"

"It's okay, baby," Mandy said, even though she had no idea if it was. Through the slit of Jordie's window, Mandy could hear the woman's ragged breaths between her thrusts against the car. Mandy fumbled to put the car into drive. You could tell from the animal look in the woman's eyes—her sunglasses had shifted halfway down her nose—that she wasn't seeing anything, not anything real.

But Mandy hadn't gone for the knife that day in the kitchen. In the instant she had to make up her mind and act, she couldn't do it, because Jordie would see. Jordie had seen plenty as it was. She shifted the car back into park, let her hands fall into her lap.

The woman's shouts and the sounds of her fists drowned out all other noise and Mandy's vision blurred. What she thought she saw was the kitchen floor and her own blood and her husband's shoes kicking their daughter away. Would principals' offices still call home every week if Jordie had witnessed an act of self-defense instead? Mandy had no idea. Grabbing the knife from the counter was the wrong thing, and so was not grabbing it. Running this woman down with her car was the wrong thing, and so was not running her down.

In her car seat, Jordie curled forward and braced her arms around her ears. Her little body rocked backward and forward almost imperceptibly. Mandy couldn't sit here letting things happen. Not again. She threw her door open, knocking the woman backward a few steps.

The woman regained her footing and reared up into Mandy's face. "What do you think you're doing?"

Mandy's jaw ached from grinding her teeth together so tight. "What do you want? You want to smack me around in front of my child? You wouldn't be the first. You want to smash up my face and leave me for dead on the street? Let some paramedics clean up your mess?" With each question, Mandy stomped another step closer to the woman. "Bring it on, asshole. I've had worse days than this."

"What the fuck is wrong with you?" The woman staggered backward.

Mandy became aware of cars braking and pulling over. People whipped out cell phones to film them. "I said bring it on." She jutted her jaw toward the woman and patted it. "Right here. Is that what you need to do? Hit me before you go away? Get it over with then."

Behind her, a loud knocking startled Mandy. She jerked around to see Jordie, loose from her car seat, frantically banging the window. The woman took her chance and stepped backward a few more paces before sprinting away down a side street.

Pamela's throat hurt and her body pulsed with heat. Each step away gave her one more breath back. She started to notice the sky again. The oranges and reds of leaves on the trees.

Eventually she had to go back for her car, but she wanted the crowds to thin first. Give the cops who were just arriving time to leave the scene. Assuming she had remembered to shut her door, her beat-up old Honda would look like any other parked car for as long as she left it there.

A public library appeared around the next corner. Pamela hurried toward it and heaved open its front door. In the restroom mirror, her hair looked like wild animals had wrestled in it, and her eyes looked used up. She fluffed her hair and re-shaped it, splashed it with a few drops of water to tame the frizz. Her shirt hung lopsided, so she evened it. Once she felt tidy enough, she'd buy some bagels from the shop by the university and catch a bus to work. She'd serve Dr. Bradshaw bagels with a side of lies about car trouble and hope today wouldn't be the day he'd fire her.

With the edge of a paper towel, she wiped smeared lipstick and smoothed what was left of her other makeup, then studied her fixed-up face. Ray used to hold this face in both hands and promise her everything. Losing him felt only half as bad as losing track of whatever it was he'd seen when he looked at her then.

Her hands were red where she'd bashed them against that car. Her bones felt crushed. She ran them under cold water until all feeling seemed to wash out of them.

Jordie kept banging, long after the woman disappeared, while onlookers cheered from their cars. One squeezed out a slightly open car door, pointing to her cell phone. "We called the police. You need anything else?"

Mandy scoffed and shook her head. "I wouldn't know where to start."

"I'm so sorry."

"Of course you are." Mandy touched her scar and slipped back into the driver's seat. Air pumped her lungs full again, as if she'd been holding her breath for hours. When her hands stopped shaking, she placed them back on the steering wheel and checked Jordie in the rearview. Quiet now, she crept back into her car seat. Mandy watched her small hands work the buckle together.

"You okay, kiddo?"

What could she say? I'm never okay? I'm always okay? The first sirens kicked up a distant wail.

From the backseat, Jordie's voice sounded miles away. "What if that woman hadn't run off? What were you going to do?"

Mandy twisted around to look directly at her. She considered lying, claiming she had the perfect plan and that everything would've ended up fine no matter what, but she said, "I don't know, Jordie. I wanted to keep us safe, but I didn't know how." Jordie's nod was full of a cynical wisdom that choked the air back out of Mandy's lungs.

A single brown leaf spiraled onto the windshield. A woman walked by with a golden retriever. In the backseat, Jordie drew the next animal cracker from the box. Sirens grew louder. Mandy didn't want to tell this story again, so she signaled and eased back onto the road toward home, as if they hadn't stopped at all.

Beautiful Day

It's Daggett's dog-walking business that brings him back to his old neighborhood for the first time in five years. The client had a family emergency and overnighted him a set of keys on the strength of his Yelp reputation, skipping his usual orientation visit, so the last time he saw this house the stucco was still brown or yellow. Not the Martha Stewart turquoise it is now, with white trim and a bright red door, looking more like a candy flavor than a house. His old street is parallel to this one, and his house and the Slocums', the one he grew up in more than his own, pull at him like water sucked to a drain.

The dogs bark from inside as he makes his way up the walk. On the porch, he shakes the keys and they yap even louder. Schnoodles, the client told him on the phone, a specialty breed that sounds to Daggett like a dressed-up word for shit. "You can check their collars to tell which is which," the client had said, which seems funny now, as the identical doggie pom-poms popcorn in the entryway in front of him. They look exactly alike, down to their black nub noses, but Daggett likes his job, so he takes time to pat their moppy heads and checks their names on the bone-shaped ID tags—Penny and Gert—before he latches his leashes onto their collars.

He brings his own because people's leashes are never where they say and he hates digging through their stuff to find them. The bright orange leashes match his polo shirt, which has "Hoos Got Your Dog" embroidered in navy thread where a breast pocket would go. Everybody's as UVA-crazy over in Waynesboro as they are here in Charlottesville, so businesses with Hoos or Cavaliers in the title automatically draw more customers. Plus, in the upscale neighborhoods, it pays to have something like a uniform for when security vans tail him and ask what he's doing there.

Not long after his parents split town for South Carolina and he bailed for cheaper rents on the other side of Afton Mountain, he kicked off the dog walking as a weekend or vacation service for travelers. At first he did it for extra cash, to boost what he made working with a team of contractors around Waynesboro. Over time, though, walking dogs grew into a full-time gig, and now wealthy folks call him from all the way over here in Charlottesville. Mostly country club types, doctors and stiff-necked lawyers. Dogs with haircuts fancier than people's and breeds that take ten minutes to explain.

He never expected a call from his old neighborhood.

The schnoodles strain at the leashes and Daggett follows, feeling like a piece of yesterday walking into today. Long before his folks moved, the houses in this neighborhood had begun the slow switch from student rentals back into the starter homes they surely were when they were built in the 40s and 50s. Now nothing's quite the same as it used to be, everything glossier and newer. He imagines his own old house with shined up floors and solar panels. Or fancy decking and an extra story glommed on top. He closes his eyes a second, to picture it the way it used to be.

A jogging stroller startles him, and his eyes flick open. He has to sidestep out of the way. The dogs skitter behind him. The stroller's one of those big-ticket models, probably cost as much as a month of Daggett's rent. The groggy baby's head bobs to the rhythm of its mother's pace while she pumps by, ears pegged to an iPhone, body sleek with spandex, and gives Daggett no more thought than the grit in the pavement. He knows the drill, spikes his glance toward the ground, further blending himself with the background.

Mica chips sparkle up at him from the asphalt, catching the sun, and sending a shiver of promise up his spine. This was his street once, and even if there's no way the Slocums still live here, their house is so close it tickles his stomach. It could be anything now, but he prefers thinking of it as its runty old self, a pale blue rancher with scalloped siding and gutters that bowed in the middle. The image that pops into his head whenever he hears the word *home*. Mr. Slocum might've asked Daggett what time he was leaving or badgered him to go bother his other friends whenever he slunk over there to dodge one of his father's rages, but Mrs. Slocum always set an extra place at their dinner table or pulled out a trundle bed at a second's notice.

Daggett learned to read late and repeated kindergarten, so he'd been the same age as Luther but the same grade as Troy, and best friends with both. Until the last summer he lived here, when Becky went from being their tagalong kid sister to whatever came next and hijacked every ounce of his attention. She was almost seventeen and he was almost twenty, and life was almost perfect for a little while.

He rounds the corner onto Robertson, his old street, but the feel of the intersection is wrong. For his entire growing-up life, a long-neglected boxwood hedge, taller than he was, lined this corner. Today, their earthy beetle odor still hangs in the air, and Penny and Gert sniff wildly at torn up ruts of land where the dead dregs of their roots tangle in the dirt. The second he turns his eyes away from those, his house looms into view, only two up from the corner.

Everything about it is updated and tidier. Their old silvered white siding swapped for stone-gray Hardie-plank. The makeshift vegetable patch at the far end of the yard now a bulb garden flaring with irises. The only out-of-place thing is a red wagon jackknifed on the front walk. A bird sings from the porch roof and a bush blooms beside the front door, but still the place echoes with his dad's rants. *Lameass!* he would say, kicking at Daggett's bed on a summer morning, swaying with liquor from the night before. *Sleeping the day away.* No matter that Daggett was only sleeping off his pre-dawn newspaper route and his dad was the one always between jobs.

He thinks his mother would like the look of the place, the blue and yellow irises like little suns and skies. Whenever they talk on the phone she begs him to visit. He tells her he loves her and makes excuses about work and the long drive, but Daggett decided after his parents moved never to put himself in the same house with his father again.

Penny and Gert sniff around his old sidewalk, squat on either side of it, kick backwards once or twice, and move on. He casts a last look over his shoulder, and the windows of his old house stare out at him like empty eyes of something dead and gone.

He takes control of the leashes again and leads the dogs across the street, toward the line of dogwoods he'd helped Mrs. Slocum plant ages ago. He remembers them from their scraggly start, half a dozen baby trees struggling toward the sunshine. Now bright pink blossoms cluster so thickly they block the house and yard from view, though he imagines seeing straight through to the front stoop and Becky standing there, barefoot, winking at him in the sunlight. Picturing her, right there where they used to be together, feels like swallowing a rock.

———————

When Becky told him she was pregnant, he would've asked her to marry him if she'd given him a chance. All she asked for was money and a ride. He sat in the waiting room, thumbing every magazine on the side table with the chipped veneer, sweat from his hands making the pages damp.

"Wait for me, Mattie?" she whispered before she left him there. The rest of the world settled on his last name by the time he was eight or nine, but with Becky he was always Mattie or Matthew. That summer, the way her t-shirt hugged her breasts. The way she walked real slow, like she knew he was watching her go by. The way she flicked her hair out of her eyes with a quick twitch of her neck. More than anything, the way she called him Mattie. Breathed his name into his ear, like she was breathing his life right into him.

On the ride home, she slumped against the passenger door of his old Le Sabre, torn vinyl spreading out from where her hands tucked under her head. Daggett steered with one hand and stroked the other against her arm. She looked like she was in pain, and he hated that he'd done something that hurt her. "I'm so sorry, Beck."

"I'm not sorry," she said. "Not about us, Mattie." She stole a look straight at him, then looked out the window again. "But I don't think I'm ready for this anymore." She shrank more toward the door and away from his touch.

This was the chance he missed to tell her how he felt, and that sad silent drive was their last time alone. He wishes he'd put up more of a fight, because how else could she have known he wanted to? He wishes at least his car had been nicer, had smelled better than dirt and gasoline and all the newspapers he delivered back then. He wishes he'd driven them past the street where they lived, hopped on a highway and kept going.

They could be going still.

Hesitating at the line of dogwoods, Daggett tries to imagine the Slocums' house as anything but what he knows. When he finally lets himself peek, he's relieved to find it's hardly changed after all. The siding is an even paler blue, drab and sickly compared to the prettified houses around it. The sagging gutters sprout shoots of green weeds. The yard is more dirt than grass like always too, from dogs tromping back and forth on it, wearing anything green to a muddy death, digging up anything else. Except for those dogwoods.

An odor lifts up from the ground that brings back the familiar dankness of the Slocums' cellar, where he and Luther and Troy used to sneak hits off the bong they stashed under forgotten, half-cracked terra cotta pots down there. That last summer, Becky crept down to join them, and suddenly Daggett noticed the littlest things about her. The way her braided rope bracelets stood out bright against her tan skin. How thick and long her eyelashes were. How close she sat to him on the upturned half barrel on the cold concrete floor. How heat spread from where her thigh pressed into his.

A couple years ago, he heard Mr. Slocum had keeled over from a heart attack out of the blue and Mrs. Slocum was selling the house. His stomach lurched at the news, like plunging down a roller coaster. The loss of the house troubled him far more than the loss of Mr. Slocum. Daggett likes to think it was a bolt of lightning to his heart, some drastic act of God declaring him unfit for this world. Without him, Daggett can't help but think he and Becky would still be together. They would've had their little baby. Maybe another one by now.

It's been almost six years, and he's dated other people, but nothing's stuck.

He hopes Mrs. Slocum got a good price.

———

The way Daggett always thinks about it is that even the abortion he got for her wasn't good enough. He had watched from his bedroom window as the EMTs lifted her into the ambulance later that night. He heard the Slocums' panicked shouts to each other as they slammed into one of their own cars to follow behind it. He sat at his window the whole night, willing them to come back, willing for none of it to have happened in the first place.

Afterward Luther explained it wasn't the abortion at all. She mistook appendicitis for the cramping the Planned Parenthood nurse warned her about. It took her until she was white with pain, almost passed out, her appendix bursting before she admitted anything was wrong and told her parents what had happened. Luther said his dad spat Daggett's name like a curse, blaming him as much as Daggett still blames himself. Never mind that Becky was only in the hospital for a couple weeks. By the end of summer, it was like nothing had happened.

He couldn't know that at the time, and for the first few days, he kept watch for when Mr. Slocum's car was gone and stopped by the house. Mrs. Slocum's car was there, but he didn't know if she'd be home or if she'd driven to the hospital with her husband. He brought a tomato cucumber salad, thinking he could leave it there with a note if no one was home. If Mrs. Slocum was the one to find it, she'd likely appreciate the gesture and at least she wouldn't throw it away.

But she was home.

"Mom wanted me to bring this by," Daggett said, even though he'd made it himself. He was ashamed to stand in front of her now that she knew about the abortion and how he and Becky had been sneaking around against Mr. Slocum's wishes all summer. He nudged the salad toward her. "From her garden."

Mrs. Slocum sat on an old metal stool at her kitchen counter and gazed at him through tired eyes. A cigarette turning all the way to ash hung from her hand. "Ain't that sweet," she said without emotion. "Put it in the fridge, if you don't mind."

Casseroles crowded into each other from a few other neighbors who didn't know what else to do either. Daggett took the time to pull them out and restack everything so it was less of a mess.

"Y'all been spending all day at the hospital, huh?" He scuffed his torn Converse sneakers against the fake-brick linoleum instead of looking up at her, afraid he might find out she was finally as fed up with him as her husband always was.

"Yeah, baby, lotta time at the hospital." She crushed the cigarette into a jar lid on the counter already full of butts. She'd been pretty once, and the way she held herself showed she remembered what that felt like. Her hair had been blond a long time ago, but now it was some yellow from a box, her skin fake-tanned, bright pink fake nails, all chipped.

"Must be rough." Dishes stacked one on top of the other in the sink like they were climbing to get out. The faucet dripped.

"You can say that again, Little Man." Her nickname for him and a sign she didn't hate him. Daggett had been the smallest of him and the Slocum boys when they were kids, and he'd started high school at a shrimpy 5'2." By graduation, he was all the way up to 5'11," but he'd always be Little Man to Mrs. Slocum.

Outside Baxter yipped. He was a sad type of dog, turned lonely before you got out the door to leave him. "I could come walk y'all's dogs for you, if you wanted," he said. "Ain't much, but that way you could take your time, you know, with Becky. Not have to rush home."

"Thanks," Mrs. Slocum said, "but they got the yard." She sounded unsure, though. She loved that little Baxter. Days off from work, she'd sit out in the yard with him wound up in her lap. Sip iced tea, gossip with the neighbors, read the newspaper sometimes, cuddling that little dog all the while.

"I could feed 'em too."

"You sure you got time for something like that?"

"Sure," Daggett said. "I got time."

A whine from the yard, and Penny and Gert's whole bodies start waggling. A chorus of mutual yips and, suddenly, here come the same old Slocum dogs, as if rising from the dirt. They hobble their way toward the fence to greet him. Five years older now, arthritic and slow, but unmistakable.

First, Baxter, Mrs. Slocum's favorite, part-dachshund, part mystery dog, reaches the fence and jumps and barks with the sound of a turkey gobble. Next comes Wallace, Daggett's favorite, a hound mutt with a pit-bull-looking head. He lumbers close to the fence and rams his fat skull into Daggett's outstretched hand, slobbering against his fingers. The touch of his sun-warm head fills Daggett with more feelings than he can keep up with.

The whole idea for his business came from taking care of the Slocums' dogs right before he moved away. To this day there's something nearly holy to him about caring for people's dogs. This shows even in the way he steps around their houses, making sure not to track mud, replacing food and water dishes exactly where he finds them. Not that anyone's watching. Judging by his Yelp reviews, people seem to know anyway.

Maybe it was easier to recognize nothing here, to believe the past was all the way past. He leans against the fence and lets the sun-hot metal burn through his shirt. Penny and Gert jam their noses through the chain link, desperate for Baxter and Wallace to notice them instead of him, but the old dogs sit back now, quiet, the excitement of hello having gone by. They fix Daggett with their soulful eyes and let out an occasional begging whine, as if they still expect, after all these years, that he's come to feed them.

"Little Man!"

The familiar voice makes Daggett jolt in surprise. Mrs. Slocum, in a tattered yellow housecoat, hurries toward him from the house. Nursing assistant at a nearby assisted living center, she's always kept odd hours, and of course he should've expected her, with nothing changed and the dogs still here. But with her rushing toward him he feels more out of time and place than ever.

She looks happy to see him, and her voice, graveled from so many years of cigarettes, manages to sound warm. "Little Man! Look at you!" She wraps both her hands around one of his across the rim of the fence. Her nails still flash bright with polish, but her dye job is paler, and her lips pinch with a wrinkle or two he doesn't remember from before. "What's it been? Five years? Six?" She plucks at the logo on his shirt. "What's this? You a businessman now?"

"I guess you could say so." He tells her a little about the dog walking. Without meaning to, he even tells her about his good Yelp reviews.

"I knew it. I knew you had it in you to do something for yourself."

"Thank you, ma'am. That's nice of you to say."

"So polite." Mrs. Slocum brushes at the air in front of her with one hand. "You don't have to be so formal, son." Baxter wags his tail at her feet, and she can't resist him long before she scoops him into her hands and smooths his velvet ears between her fingers. "Let me get you a coffee or something." She scrapes the gate open. It half-sticks in the semi-circle rut of bare dirt leftover from years of opening and closing.

She links her free arm through his to lead him into the yard, then drags the gate shut behind them and drops Baxter back onto the ground. She unclips Penny and Gert's leashes too, without asking, so all the dogs can romp the yard together. In his head, his dad's voice shouts *Lameass*. He usually keeps his work dogs separate from regular ones, and he has other clients to get to, but Mrs. Slocum keeps pulling.

The Slocums' kitchen looks cleaner now, with fresh yellow paint on the walls and a fresh coat of white on the cabinets, but the same pock-marked fake-brick linoleum. A low sprawling plant seems to uncoil itself in strands at the window over the sink. Mrs. Slocum rattles drawers and cabinets, gathering grounds and filters and mugs.

"I haven't seen as much as your shadow since your folks left the street, Little Man."

"I've been living on the other side of the mountain," Daggett says. "Time sure has gone by."

"Ain't that the truth. Do you know I'm a grandma now? Luther's a daddy. Got two babies. Both girls, one and three."

The Mr. Coffee puffs and coughs. Mrs. Slocum fingers the spoon handles. "Different mamas, God bless him. He changes jobs some, but he seems like he's getting closer to settled down. And would you believe Troy done moved out West? Denver. Working for a moving company."

"Is that right?" Daggett resists making a joke about the mile-high city being a good place for him. Troy would've laughed, though. "I thought he was in Florida."

"He's been a long time gone from there, son. Such a shame y'all fell out of touch." Now Mrs. Slocum lines up the mugs. The coffee pot's almost full. "You know, Becky's doing good," she says, the end of the statement sounding like a question. "She finished up at college. Now she's teaching first grade down in Roanoke."

"That's good. Real good." Becky, teaching. A passel of children at her feet, a world of chalkboards and story-books. A whole series of pictures in his head that weren't there before.

"She asks about you, time to time." Mrs. Slocum pours the coffee, slides a mug his way across the counter. With a gesture she offers milk and sugar. He takes his with nothing, pulls a hot mouthful, scalding away the rush of words that wants to tumble out. The sheer delight of knowing Becky would ever think of him. Times he'd seen her after the hospital and before he moved away, she seemed almost afraid to look at him. Like seeing him would hurt her all over again. If she spoke to him at all, she called him Daggett.

"Tell her I said hello sometime. Will you do that?"

"Sure I will."

He follows Mrs. Slocum to the Formica-topped table in the center of the room, and they both sit down. Water fizzes on the coffee maker's burner and the faucet plinks out a single drip.

"I always pictured the two of you meeting up again some-day," Mrs. Slocum says, nearly causing Daggett to choke on his next sip. "You two was sweet together."

Not something he dreamed Mrs. Slocum would ever say since the ending between them seemed destined to leave a bad taste. "Mr. Slocum sure thought different." When he'd tried to visit Becky at the hospital, her father had blocked his way at the door. Behind him, Becky's face swam up out of a swirl of white bedding, ashy as the sheets themselves. She nodded at him to go, to listen to her dad, but he hated to leave her there, stuck with their mistake and all the pain it caused.

"Mr. Slocum could be a porcupine of a man, God rest him." Mrs. Slocum glances into the yard, toward the sounds of the dogs playing with each other. "You were gentle with her. She needed that."

Daggett rests his mug on the table in front of him and spreads his palms flat on the cool tabletop. "If I could've kept her from hurting, I would've done anything."

"I know that." Mrs. Slocum pats his hand, squeezes his fingers. "Everybody knows that, Little Man. You ever look in a mirror when you saw that girl? It showed all over your face."

Embarrassed, he scans the floor, coughs. "Still, I felt like I let her down. Left her alone when I should've been there."

"I don't suppose she needed anything but time."

"I would've married her," Daggett says, "if she would've let me."

Mrs. Slocum chuckles and sits back in her chair. Her coffee sloshes in her cup. "Have you been riding around your whole grown-up life with that notion hanging around your neck? That you and Beck should've gotten married and started a family? What do you think your lives would be like now if you'd gone and done that?"

Hair falls across Daggett's eyes and he shoves it out of the way. He thinks of what their lives would be like all the time. Their kid almost old enough to be in the classroom she's teaching now.

"It took every ounce of her strength to keep from running after you when she got to feeling better. Did you know that?" Mrs. Slocum says.

"No, ma'am." Whenever Daggett had seen her, he thought she was using every ounce of her strength to forget him.

"She was the first Slocum to graduate college."

"I would've never stood in her way," Daggett says.

"Not on purpose," Mrs. Slocum says. "But Beck was just a girl back then, and truth is, I call you Little Man for more than just sprouting up later than my boys. Seems like you always had forever on your mind. Look at you now, fixed up with a business of your own, your own uniform." She pats her chest at the spot where Daggett's logo is on his. "Naw, Little Man, if y'all had gone off and got married, all y'all'd have now is a kid or two and a lifetime of debt. You'd be doggy paddling your lives away."

Until this moment, Daggett's life had seemed like a rope that losing Becky had sliced in half, and he'd struggled ever since to cinch the ends back together. He swigs a gulp of coffee that lands in his belly like acid. The two ends don't fit back together. He should've realized that a long time ago. If he and Beck met in the street today, they'd have to start over, like strangers.

He and Mrs. Slocum sip their coffee a little longer. She offers cookies and recites bits of news about people they used to know. But time rolls around the way it always does. He carries his dirty cup to the kitchen sink.

"I got to get on with some more dogs to walk and all, but, do me a favor, okay?" Daggett says. "Tell Becky I'm real proud of her. Will you do that?"

"I will," Mrs. Slocum says. "I'm sure she'd be real proud of you too."

They meet at the back door. "Thanks for having me," he says.

"Just like old times."

Daggett offers a hand to shake, but she pulls him to her chest instead. She holds him like a single hug could bring back all the people and things you lost in your life.

He buckles Penny and Gert back to his leashes, scrapes the Slocums' gate open and closed one last time. The dogs pull and he lets them lead again, pissing and sniffing their way back toward their own house.

The chatter of the schnoodles' claws and the way their legs seem to scissor faster than the dogs themselves make Daggett laugh to himself. Ahead of them, a pair of ludicrously little dogs turns onto the street, and Penny and Gert lunge toward them. More designer types. Miniature Yorkies, he figures. Small enough to fit in his cereal bowl. The woman walking them struggles to keep up, thin leather leashes threatening to fly from her hand.

She's small herself and smartly dressed, probably walking her dogs on her lunch break instead of hiring someone like him to do it. He assumes she'll pass him by without a glance, same as the woman with the stroller, and so many other women in neighborhoods like this one, even if this hasn't been a neighborhood like that for very long. To make it easier for her he stands aside, pretending to untangle his leashes.

Instead, when she reaches him, she smiles wide, as if she expected to run into him. She brings along the fresh smell of her soap or some other light flowery perfume. Her sunlit hair shifts in the breeze.

"It's a beautiful day, isn't it?"

The way she says it makes Daggett belong to this street again, to the wide universe, so he tips his head to look up at the crisp greenness of the trees, the clouds puffing across the swimming pool blue sky, the inky purple ridge of mountains in the distance. He can't see where it's coming from, but he smells honeysuckle or wisteria blooming somewhere.

"It sure is," he says, as if he'd just now opened his eyes after a long time keeping them shut against the world.

Damage

David's cell phone vibrated, his old landline number flashing on its screen. He had stayed late to crunch numbers with his boss ahead of their quarterly meeting. Interrupting with a call from his ex would cost him credibility. He pictured Trudy with the phone cradled against a shoulder, leaning against the sink in their old kitchen, glaring at the clock on the wall. She hated waiting for him. His phone buzzed again.

"Do you think I'm calling to *chat*?" she'd snap after he ignored a call, as if chatting were the most disgusting of possibilities. It was true she didn't call often, and when she did it was usually important. Once, work made him skip the call when their older daughter Ginnie broke her leg at a track meet. Work also made him forget the meet.

Finally, David risked annoying his boss and answered.

"Smoke's coming in under the door. What do I do?" It was his younger daughter, Layna, just turned thirteen.

"Smoke? God, Layna. Are you by yourself?" No answer on the other end, only Layna, breathing fast, and the smoke alarm's syncopated shriek. The office and his boss's face blurred into the background.

"It's coming in under the front door. I don't know what to do."

"Get out of the house, Layna. Go to the back door."

David's boss's eyebrows tented in alarm and he grabbed for his own phone, started dialing. David stayed on the line while Layna walked through the house. His heart pumped double-time, but he kept his voice calm. "Go to our safe spot. Remember?" Back in her elementary school days, the school sent a paper home during fire prevention week outlining safety steps. Draw up a plan. Schedule family fire drills. Keep fire extinguishers in the kitchen and upstairs. The regimen had sounded alarmist to David at the time, but misfiring smoke detectors had given them plenty of practice anyway. Their safe spot was the dogwood tree at the edge of the cul-de-sac in their front yard.

"Are you there?" The phone went dead.

His boss had a dispatcher on the line, and David relayed his old address while gathering his files and notes from the desk out of reflex. His boss repeated the address into the phone and waved David out of the office. Just like Trudy used to tell him, "You don't get fired for having a family, David. Jesus."

From his car, he tried calling Layna again, but the line rolled over to voicemail. Same thing happened when he tried Ginnie and Trudy.

Past rush hour, the traffic was thin but unnerving. Too-long red light here, slow driver there. The world seemed full of obstacles and idiots.

Most times, he was the idiot. He had no idea what prompted Layna to call him today instead of her mom who Mary Poppins-ed her way through parenting, unfazed by whatever illness or hazard came their way. He was determined not to let Layna down the way he had before the separation, like the time a late meeting made him forget to pick her up from an after-school club. The assistant principal had finally driven her home, then waited with her on the front steps until someone else got there. Of course Trudy arrived first; she always got home from work on time. Where was she tonight?

Fire engines crowded the street in front of David's old house. Flashing red lights sliced in and out of the dark. Dissipating smoke around the front porch shimmered in lifting red clouds. In the yard, firefighters shouted back and forth and re-rolled lengths of hose.

The sirens squawked to a stop an instant before David got out of his car, but the lights kept strobing. The neon strips on a firefighter's uniform caught the glare of David's headlights, and he finally saw Layna, beside him, crouching at the base of the dogwood tree. The way Layna huddled there made her look half her thirteen years at best.

David ran and stooped beside her, hugging her and saying her name over and over. A thick wool blanket draped her shoulders, something the firefighter must have given her.

"Here's what we know," the firefighter said. "Your daughter here's fine, but pretty shook up. No one else was home. Looks like somebody stuck a smoke bomb between the storm door and the front door. Wouldn't have done much on its own, but trapped that way it made a mess. Nothing caught fire. We're looking at damage, making sure that's all there was. Should be okay for y'all to head back inside any minute."

David's other daughter Ginnie jogged up as the firefighter went to rejoin his crew in the yard. "Dad?" She seemed as surprised to see him as she was to see the fire engines. She bent over her little sister. "Are you okay?"

Next on the scene, Trudy screeched her car to a halt in the cul-de-sac and bolted out of it, scanning the dark yard and calling, "Girls? Dear God. Girls?"

David shouted, "Over here!" and Trudy's hand dropped across her heart, the first time she'd been relieved to see him in longer than he could remember. But for the emergency vehicles, they'd look like the perfect tableau of a family to anyone passing by, with Layna leaning into his arms, Ginnie standing behind him—one hand on his shoulder, one hand trailing softly through Layna's hair—and Trudy completing their circle.

A firefighter shouted from the porch, "Y'all can go on inside now. House is clear." Another motioned them toward the back door, away from the huddle inspecting the front door. A smoky funk hung in the air. David and his family climbed the deck stairs to the back door.

Inside, the funky smell was fainter. Smudges on the white rugs showed where firefighters' boots had trod, helter-skelter, as they searched the house for other dangers. In the living room, Trudy settled into the overstuffed chair, doing her best to cradle Layna in her lap.

For the six months of their separation, Trudy had controlled the girls' pick-ups and drop-offs so completely that David hardly made it past the foyer anymore. The living room felt unfamiliar now, with a new sofa, new TV, and even the old end tables in new places. When everyone began talking about what happened, David felt shoved to the sidelines, as if he hadn't been there too.

"I was at the grocery store," Trudy said. "I'd left my cell phone charging."

Ginnie said, "I was hanging out at Lisa's," her friend down the block, "and I saw fire trucks zooming up to our end of the street. I didn't really think they could be for us, but Layna was alone so I took off running anyway."

"I called Mom and I could hear her phone ringing. Right over there," Layna said and pointed toward the island separating the living room and kitchen. David looked, but couldn't see a phone among all the books and after-school snack dishes yet to be cleared. Now he knew why she'd called him first.

"A smoke bomb?" Trudy said, as if the news had just hit her. "This was meant as some kind of joke?" Her eyes met David's. Layna and Ginnie looked to him too. He wanted to give them answers, assurances, but he didn't know what to say.

Instead, he said, "Are there groceries in the car?" He knew what to do with groceries.

Outside, David threaded his way from the backyard then down the sidewalk to where Trudy's car stood, door yawning open, keys still hanging from the ignition. He grabbed the keys, gathered the bags, locked the doors, and headed back toward the house. From the porch a firefighter shouted to let him know he could use the front door again.

"Looks like all cosmetic damage," he told David as he made his way up the steps. "You're looking at a couple new doors, maybe some wood for the threshold. Nothing structural, though."

David thanked him and shouldered past him through the door. Inside, bright lights from idling fire trucks pulsed red down the white hallway. Layna still clung to her mother. Ginnie sat across from them on the sofa, talking on her phone about the prank. "Some asshole, getting off on scaring my little sister."

Layna shivered against her mother. Weird how feelings could outlast their causes. Unloading groceries in the kitchen helped David hide it, but he was shaking too. It had only been a smoke bomb, but when Layna called, all he had known was that something bad had happened, and he hadn't been here to stop it. Bad things would happen again and again, and he would never be here to stop it because he lived somewhere else now.

He busied himself in the kitchen as long as he could, moving on to dirty snack dishes as soon as he finished emptying grocery bags. When a knock came at the door, David told Trudy he'd get it. It was Mark, a police officer they knew from a few streets over. David wondered if he'd heard about the divorce. He was on duty now, though. They stood in the foyer to talk.

"Some neighbor kid with a police scanner app heard Dispatch call in the response for your house. Saw some boys running off down the street and recognized them," Mark said. He mentioned which boys they were. "You know them, David. Good families, decent kids."

The boys had lived in the neighborhood for ages, played ball at the end of this street sometimes, just started getting acne and forgetting how to talk around Ginnie. They were a little rowdy, but they knew how to flash boy-next-door smiles and say, "Yes, sir," in time to stay this side of trouble.

"What they wanted," Mark said, "was for the smoke to spook Ginnie enough so she'd run outside. Give them a look at her and something to talk about." Laugh lines crinkled Mark's eyes. "You believe that? Bunch of goofballs."

David believed it. At sixteen, Ginnie looked twenty—pouty lips, grownup curves, and enough confidence to tie the tongues of most pubescent boys. For the smoke bomb stunt, David guessed, the cluster of boys would have crouched behind the rose of Sharon at the edge of the sidewalk, phones poised to record. Best case scenario, Ginnie would've chased them down and begged them not to post it, and somehow they would've all ended up laughing. Harmless enough, but the thought of those lanky, zit-pocked teenagers scheming for a sneak peek at his daughter cramped David's stomach. Worse was knowing that, if he'd thought of it way back when, he might have tried the same kind of prank on Ruth Bentley on Jackson Street, too pretty to talk to him when he was just fifteen. He wouldn't have thought any more than these boys did about little sisters or smoke damage or what right he had to look in the first place.

Layna, home alone, with smoke seeping in under the front door and those boys outside waiting. How long before they realized they'd scared up the wrong sister? Too young yet to get their kind of humor, if anyone ever really did get it. Had they had the nerve to be disappointed, watching her scramble, terrified, toward the dogwood while they loped away, unscathed?

"So, whaddaya think, Dave, maybe you get them boys down here to help fix up the damage? Pay for it and do the work too? They keep their records clean and you get them to put everything back the way it was?"

David didn't answer. Who in this world gets to put things back the way they were?

Mark noticed David's hesitation, took a step back as if to make physical space for a different opinion. "Hey, we can send up charges to the juvenile court if that's what you want. But I'll tell you, that big kid, Dylan? I come to the door, he's got tears in his eyes. Keeps asking if everybody's okay. He never guessed anybody'd call 9-1-1, and when he saw those fire engines, he figured the whole house was burning down. I'll be honest, man, I let him ask about four times before I told him everybody was okay. The rest of those boys hung behind Dylan, too scared to move. They know they screwed up, if you're worried about that."

"Yeah, I'm worried about that," David said.

Trudy must have managed to slide Layna from her lap. She joined David and Mark in the foyer. Mark brought her up to date about the boys and the offer for them to fix things up instead of going to court. With a look, Trudy seemed to defer the decision to David, even though she didn't do that anymore. A few weeks ago, he had offered to replace the spotlight over the garage when he'd noticed it was out, and she'd fussed about how it was her house now and he had to quit acting like it wasn't. It was fixed now too, beaming a steady yellow swath of light that the fire engines' red lights kept crisscrossing.

Trudy letting him help felt good, so he thought hard about what was best. In the end, it was nothing more than a smoke bomb. It wasn't supposed to cause a fire, and it hadn't. Some things, when they were meant to be small, or nothing at all, deserved second chances. So David said, "Okay. The boys can help fix it."

Trudy nodded, accepting his decision. "You'll have to work with them, though, David. I don't want to see them."

About the same time Mark left, the fire engines' lights flashed off, leaving behind a moment's reddish afterglow in the darkness. Warning beeps sounded, and the trucks finally backed out and away from the house.

In the living room, Layna curled against her mother again. It was seven-forty-five on a school night. David said, "I'm calling out for pizza. It's late and we're all hungry." This time Trudy's look seemed to say that she wouldn't have deferred a decision about pizza to him. He had outstayed his usefulness.

Later, answering the door, David noticed the pizza guy checking out the smoke damage. He joked, "Yeah, it's been a hot night in here." The pizza guy looked at him funny, as if even he could tell David didn't live here anymore.

The pizza left a sheen on David's hands and tautened his stomach like a sore muscle. When it was gone, he knew it was time for him to leave. By then the pizza smell had subsided, and the sulfur after-stench from the smoke bomb reeked throughout the house in its place. Layna already looked as if she'd been up for three days straight, and David couldn't imagine her falling asleep tonight in a house that stunk of smoke bomb.

He dragged a hand across his face, wondered if he looked as tired as Layna. "Why don't you all come back to my house tonight?" he said. "That way, even though it'll be cold, you could leave some windows open here, air the place out."

Trudy considered his offer, but David knew, even if she wanted to come, she'd talk herself out of it. She was letting him help today only because it was best for the girls, not because she missed him. Not because she woke up mornings, twisted in the sheets, aching for the feel of his flesh, the smell of his hair.

"I'll be fine here, David," Trudy said, and he knew she would be. "But the girls can go with you if they want."

Ginnie was sitting beside her mother on the sofa, texting one of her friends. She became aware of the conversation around her and tucked the phone into her pocket. "Are you sure you'll be all right?" she asked her mother.

"I'm sure." Trudy leaned over and kissed Ginnie's forehead.

At some point, David had stopped doing that, kissing their foreheads, their cheeks. He thought if he did it now, it would be weird. They used to climb into his lap, wet from bathtimes, smelling like flowers. He would burrow his nose into their wet hair, tickle their sides, smother their little bellies in raspberries.

David's house smelled the same as it always did, of sawdust and a faint odor of new paint. The girls unloaded into it the way they always did too, like visitors, carrying duffel bags and leaving their shoes neatly at the door. His leather sofa exhaled under them as they sank into the cushions, balancing their schoolbooks in their laps to finish the homework they had all nearly forgotten. Layna hooked her phone into David's music system, and her favorite pop bands clanged their unfamiliar sounds into the air. No wonder she and Ginnie spent all their time with him texting friends and playing games on their phones. There was nothing about this house that felt like it belonged to them.

But it didn't smell like a smoke bomb. So when bedtime came around, they got ready as if it were a normal night. David leaned into each of their doorways to say good night. The girls peeked out at him from underneath bedspreads they'd had when they were younger. He had thought the old spreads would make their rooms feel homey, but now he could see they just made the rooms seem out of date.

David stayed up late in bed, going through the papers he had stuffed into his briefcase hours before, so he was awake to hear the light shuffle of Layna's footsteps around midnight. He peered into the hall and watched her walk slowly to the top of the steps, crane forward, as if she were listening for something, then feel her hand along the wall there.

"Layna?" he whispered, trying not to startle her, but she gasped and whipped her neck around toward him anyway. That fire prevention program had also trained the children how to check if your house was on fire. One way was to go to the top of the stairs and listen, then test the walls for heat. "Honey, what're you doing?"

"Nothing," she said, but she didn't move her hand from the wall.

"Sweetheart, there's no fire." He was beside her now, pulling her close. "There's no fire." He left his papers strewn across his bed and unrolled a sleeping bag onto the floor of Layna's room. Twice that night, she woke up screaming. David reached his hand up to the side of the bed, and Layna clutched onto it, long after they both fell asleep again.

Two weeks later when the boys came to fix the doors, they brought some tools and money to pay for the supplies David provided. He showed them the new front door, the new storm door, the custom-cut strip of wood for the threshold, and the woodwork that needed sanding, priming, and re-painting. He explained how to do each task and how he'd supervise to make sure their work was proper and precise. They kept serious looks on their faces and said, "Yes, sir, Mr. Weld."

It was early April now, sunny and unseasonably hot. The boys worked without complaining. David was surprised. About halfway through, he told them, "You know, you're doing a really good job."

"Thanks, Mr. Weld." The boys grinned. "We didn't mean any trouble."

Their grins hit him wrong. They were angling to make good with him, maybe practicing for when they hoped to pick Ginnie up for a date sometime. They probably didn't know David wouldn't be the parent to answer this door they were re-building together.

Every now and then, Ginnie's curtain flapped upstairs. He had told her to find something else to do, but she had overheard how these boys had pulled this prank just to catch sight of her. Now she was trying to catch sight of them, their muscles gleaming with sweat, working to make things right.

Too soon, the job was finished. A little sanding and hammering and painting, and that was it. The boys began packing up their things. They lined up, right by the dogwood tree, the family's safe spot where David had found Layna that day. One of the boys tried to tell David goodbye or thank you, and David tried to think of something to say that would matter more than the work they had done. He became aware of the sun bearing down on them, burning the flesh of his neck, and he wished it had been hotter, that the work had been harder.

"Layna has nightmares," he said, because she did, even if he only knew about them because Trudy told him. One at a time, he looked each boy in the eye. "She wakes up screaming, thinking the house is burning down." The boys turned away from him, all their grins gone, and they sought out spots along the sidewalk where they could look without meeting his eyes. "Every night."

Above them, Ginnie's bedroom window whooshed open. "Hey, assholes! Next time just knock on the damn door!" Then she slammed the window shut. Her laughter rang through the glass. Even Layna was giggling. Snarky smiles flashed across the boys' faces, like they'd gotten what they wanted from the beginning, and they swaggered down the street.

Scraps of smoke-damaged threshold lay at David's feet. He lifted one into his hand, slapped it against his open palm once, twice, then shouted, "Hey, boys!" Their smiles dissolved into looks of confusion and fear as David hurled the shard of wood straight at them. Then they broke into sloppy sprints and barreled out of sight.

Grown-Up Party

It's hot outside and her father is driving too fast. On the radio, "Do the Hustle" switches to a report of a missing child. Eight years old, just like her. Lost walking home from a friend's house in a nearby neighborhood. Her father's cigarette ash creeps toward his fingers then breaks. The AC vent spews it in her direction. Dana flicks the flakes from her sunburned thigh and goes back to looking out the window.

"You can't spend every minute with your friend, Dana," her father says, continuing the argument she lost before she got into his car to go to this grown-up party. "You're here to visit me."

"Shake Your Booty" fades in. In the back seat her older brother thwacks his new boomerang against his palm. Every now and then he snaps it so the plastic blade swings up between the inside of the car door and the edge of the front seat, jabbing the back of her arm. She swats after it like it's a bug.

At Corrie's, they play stuffed animals and sing along with the radio. Corrie's mom makes bread from scratch and sometimes rubs their shoulders at bedtime when Dana sleeps over. Nobody pokes at her with anything or punishes her for wanting to play with her friend. It's always quiet at their house and calm. For that matter, it's always calm and quiet back at her own house with her own mother, and there she and Alec can go to the neighborhood pool every day, except for Mondays when it's closed, and she's allowed to bring library books wherever they go. Her mom knows she won't lose them.

Her dad side-eyes his own reflection in the corner of the rearview mirror and pats a hand against his wavy hair. Dana slinks closer to the passenger door, rests her face against the vinyl. Alec pops the boomerang into her arm again.

"Quit it." If she twists her neck and strains her gaze around the edge of her seat, she can see a sliver of his googly expression. He sticks out his tongue. Three years older and he acts like a baby.

Their father pulls into a parking space on a street of townhouses. These are taller and more modern looking than the brick ones where they live with their mother, two hours away. Across the street a man in sunglasses leans against his car. If he's coming to the same party, he's not in any hurry. He's wearing a silky disco shirt like from Soul Train and faded blue jeans. He doesn't seem to notice them.

Her father plants his feet on the pavement and his keys jangle in his hands, clicking against his lighter. He sparks his next brown cigarette into action. Ash speckles his mustache. Alec tumbles out of the car and rushes to walk beside him, edging Dana out of the way.

She's caught her brother peeking at himself in the bathroom mirror at home. He tiptoes so he can lean around the sink and scrunch his face up close to the glass, then he tucks his upper lip tight to his front teeth to show the spot under his nose better. Checking for a mustache, even though he's only eleven. Maybe that's why he doesn't seem to mind going to a party with a bunch of grownups they don't know. Maybe she is being a baby for wanting to play with her friend instead.

Their father stops them on the sidewalk. Whenever he stares down at them, his face seems far away and Dana feels tiny and invisible. It felt like that even before, when they all lived together. "You know the rules," he says. "Keep out of trouble and keep out of the way." He uses his stern voice and glowers at them. His cigarette churns out white clouds like the smokestack between his house and their mom's that stinks like old eggs for at least a mile.

They enter through the kitchen where platters of raw hamburger and hot dogs wait for the cookout later, and trays of carrots and celery with Cheez Whiz and plastic bowls of ridged potato chips and Fritos crowd the countertops. On every surface, ashtrays overflow with nubs and soot. A radio plays in the background. Something about riding a horse through the desert.

Dana pokes through magazines on the coffee table. A couple of news ones. Ones with pictures of the insides and outsides of houses. Boring. Her dad let Alec bring his stupid boomerang, even though all he does is hit her with it, but he wouldn't let her bring a library book because he said she'd lose it. Said he didn't care what her mother let her do, she could let them run wild in the street if she wanted, but at his house it was his rules. Now he leans his back against a wall and laughs while smoke snakes out of his nostrils and up toward the ceiling. The woman he talks to wears a one-piece jumpsuit, the same green as Dana's pencils from school, with a neckline that cuts a V all the way to her waist.

Beside her Alec says, "Awww, Daaaana," in his telling-on-you voice before she focuses on the next magazine from the stack in her lap. It's like one of the nasty ones her father gets. She can't look away at first. A naked man, holding his private part. A naked woman, her mouth wide, kneeling in

front of him. Dana's entire insides turn greasy. She chucks
the magazine back onto the coffee table, but not before
Alec reaches their father, tugs his sleeve, points at her. The
boomerang wags behind him like a rigid tail.

Their father follows Alec to the coffee table. Ice clacks in
his glass. Alec grabs a corner of the magazine and says, "This
is the one." The woman their father was talking to lopes
along beside him. Her body is one long ripple. Up close,
Dana can see bare skin all the way down to her bellybutton.

"I see you found the *Penthouse*," the woman says. "Nice
choice." Her smile shows all her teeth and her bright pink
gums. "It's okay with me if you want to look at it, as long
as your dad doesn't mind."

"Sure, yeah, do what you like," he says. Alec, the tattler,
looks disappointed.

Dana's stomach fizzes. She remembers when she believed
no one could see her when she closed her own eyes, and she
wishes that could be true now, or at least that she could still
believe it. "I don't want to look."

"It's okay for girls to look too," the woman says.

"I said I don't want to," Dana says, louder this time.

"Whatever you say," the woman says. But Dana can tell
by her voice she doesn't believe her, that she's making a joke
of her answer with her father. He laughs and looks at the
bare flesh of the woman's chest. Dana can't find anything to
look at that isn't skin. The magazine, the woman, her own
arms. She screws her eyes shut.

Alec plops the boomerang onto the sofa and sits down,
then slides the magazine into his own lap. Dana would like
to be with Corrie, playing with Basil the rabbit and Dorinda
the elephant. She would like to do anything but sit here
with grownups talking about nasty magazines. Alec's face

reddens, but he keeps looking, turning one slow page at a time. The paper sticks to his fingers.

In front of them the woman laughs at something their father said that Dana couldn't hear. She leans her whole head backward. Her hair is so long it reaches the backs of her knees. Her father stretches a finger from the rim of the drink he holds and touches her belly button. It activates her like a toy. She lurches forward again, her laugh a shriek. She almost swipes their father with the cigarette in her hand.

Then she bends low to square a look at Dana. "You're lucky to grow up in this day and age." Dana can smell her cigarette breath. The woman takes a puff and rights herself again, then lets a snail of smoke out of her mouth. "Our parents were impossible about sex, weren't they, Ricky?" She hangs a finger from her father's belt loop. "It's like they figured if they kept it secret enough we'd never be curious on our own." Then back to Dana, "You're lucky your dad's so open." When she says the word *open*, Dana can tell it means things she doesn't know about yet.

"Wide open," her father says, but not to her. The woman brushes her hand down the button front of her father's shirt.

Dana wants a piece of paper. Some crayons. She could draw with a pencil on a grocery bag. Anything. She taps her father's wrist so he lowers his head to hear her. "How much longer?"

"A lot longer. We just got here." He and the woman cross the room again, joining a couple of other people with their cigarettes and drinks.

"You don't have to look at it anymore," she says to her brother. "They're gone."

"Don't be stupid," he says. "I like it."

She grabs at his boomerang, but he whacks her hand away then shoves the magazine toward her, centerfold first.

When Dana knocks it away, it rips. "Oooh." Alec revs up his tell-on-you voice again.

People spill out of the house and onto the patch of grass out front, talking, smoking, holding drinks. Dana slips outside with them. Rows of ferns line the front of the house. June bugs divebomb Dana from the bushes that frame the porch. Gnats plink against her face.

The man with the disco shirt still leans against the car across the street, smoking a cigarette and facing away from the house. That's where Dana would like to go. Away from the house. She kicks along the sidewalk. A line of ants marches through a crack in the cement. They're carrying bits of something.

When she looks back toward the front of the house again, she sees her father, outside now too, sitting on the lawn beyond the porch. The woman in the green jumpsuit lies in the grass, her head in his lap. They say something to each other in voices she can't hear. Then her father calls, "Dana, come here."

He's still taller than she is when he's sitting down. "How old are you?" he says, the way parents of little kids ask them what a cow says.

"Eight."

"Flo here wants to know if you've ever lit a match?" Flo pokes his thigh. It's a joke again.

"I'm not allowed."

"You're allowed here." He jostles in his pockets, bouncing Flo's head about in his lap, making her laugh her terrible shriek over and over. He fishes out a matchbook. "Here. Try it."

"I don't want to."

"Aw, don't be scared," Flo says.

"Mom says not to."

"I keep telling you," her father says, "you don't have to do what she says when you're with me." Dana thinks about her library books. She'd rather do what her mother says. "Anyway, I don't want to raise you up to be a scaredy cat like her." The woman and her father smile big goofy smiles that have nothing to do with her. She wants them to leave her alone. "Go ahead." Her father presses the book into her hands. "I bet you can't." He says it like a dare.

She wants to throw the matchbook in his face, but she knows she's too little and he'd either laugh at her or get lightning-storm mad the way he does sometimes. Her brother rushes in and swats the matches out of her hand with his boomerang. "Give it here," he says and grabs them from the grass, lights one, then another.

"That's not nice," Flo says, "knocking something out of your sister's hand." She pries the book from Alec's fingers and gives it back to Dana. Even though she doesn't want it. "Here you go, Dina." Dana doesn't correct her.

Alec gives her a sour look and jams his hands into his pockets. The woman stuck up for her, so now Dana feels like she has to try the match. "You can do it. It's no big thing," she says, keeping her eyes locked on Dana's. It doesn't seem like a joke anymore. It seems like something the woman really wants to teach her. Something grown-up.

Dana tries. Nothing happens. She tries again, the match bends. She tries a new match and it catches. She's holding too close to the tip and it singes her finger. The flame jumps to the matchbook and flares. She hurls it away from herself. It lands on her father's wrist.

"Goddammit!" He jolts forward and Dana jumps back. Flo tumbles out of his lap. He stamps the flaming matchbook and waves his hand, shouting, "Jesus, Dana! What the hell?" As if it had been her idea. As if she meant to hurt him.

She spins and huffs away toward the street. "Run it under cold water, Ricky," Flo says behind her. Her father's and Flo's voices back away into the house.

Dana walks the entire length of the sidewalk. Any farther and she'll be lost. All these townhouses look exactly the same, row upon row upon row. She ambles back closer to the party again and sits on the curb across from where they parked. Near where the disco shirt man puffs smoke rings into the air.

A breeze kicks up and blows pollen around the street. Long reeds of some kind of bushes scissor the air behind her.

"Not having any fun?" It's the disco shirt man.

"Nope."

"I bet you don't want to be here at all."

He's right. But she doesn't want to say. She hugs her knees to herself. She's tired of grownups thinking they know what she wants.

All the same, he comes closer. He sits down near her on the curb. "I don't like to smoke near kids," he says, "sorry," and grinds the butt into the cement. He blows the last of his smoke away from her and flaps his hand to make it disappear faster. "I saw what they did about the match. That was a pretty dumb thing to do with a kid." A June bug buzzes between them, bumps into the man's arm. He brushes after it. "I mean, I'm sorry they made you do something you didn't want to do." The bug darts into the bushes.

Dana scrapes a stone against the street under her feet. She shrugs at the man.

"Geez, I'd never do that with a kid." The man's sunglasses are dark black so Dana can't tell what his eyes are doing, but his head aims toward the street away from her, even farther away from the party, as if he's all the time thinking of being someplace else.

Dana tightens her hold on her knees, makes herself into a ball. The noise of the party is not as loud from here, but voices rise up on a breeze, people sing-shouting along with the radio.

"Yeah, no way you want to be here," the disco shirt man says again.

"No."

"Where would you rather be?" He levers his sunglasses out of the way to look at her, and his eyes are as blue as lake water at night. "If you could pick?"

The first grownup all day to ask her what she wants instead of telling her. She looks closer at him. Scrubby sideburns. Fluffy brown hair. Crooked yellow teeth. It's really hot outside, but he's not sweating. "Anywhere," she says and gives a sly smile. Her own joke.

He laughs. "No, really. Where?"

She thinks of Corrie's house, but what she really wants is home. "I'd rather be at my mom's. But I have to wait until Sunday night for my dad to take me back."

He nods. "That must feel like a long time."

"A really long time."

"What if I could snap my fingers and send you back there this second? Would you want me to?"

Dana laughs. "You can't do that. You're not magic."

"No, but it's sort of a game, to think of things happening the way you want."

Down at the party, a whoop goes up, then a burst of laughter. People clap their hands and shout, like they're egging someone on. The sound drowns out the music.

"So, let's say I could snap my fingers. Say I am magic. Would you want me to?"

"And then I'd be home? No long car ride? No more waiting?"

The disco shirt man nods.

"Sure. I'd like that."

Disco shirt man hmms to himself, like he's mulling something over. "What's your name?"

She tells him.

"Well, Dana, you're right that I'm not magic. But know what? I do really like to drive, and I could take you home. To your mom."

"It's a long way." All the water dries up in her mouth, but she doesn't know why. She can hear the music from the party again, but it seems to warp a little. She doesn't know this song.

"That's okay. I like driving."

"You don't even know the way." Dana forces another laugh.

"I bet you know the address," he says. "Smart girl like you."

A shrill yee-haw peals across the strip of yards from the party. Her father. He pumps a fist, now on the top step of the porch with a group of them pouring something into tiny glasses and gulping them down. She doesn't know where her brother is.

"Yeah, I know my address," she says. When he flicks his head toward his car across the street and stands, she follows.

The crowd of partiers shouts and shimmies on the lawn. Dana takes a backward glance, and they look ridiculous, like something out of a cartoon, all bright colors and shapes shifting around, not like anything real.

The man opens her door for her and gestures for her to get in. Everything inside goes hot and she thinks she might throw up. Then a sound whips past her ear and she ducks out of the way. When she looks up, the man is slapping Alec's boomerang to the ground. Then he wipes the air in front of his clothes, like he's dusting something off himself. Alec bursts out of some bushes right beside where the car is parked.

"Almost got you!" he shouts at Dana. He doesn't pay any attention to the disco shirt man, who slams Dana's door and skirts around the front of the car to his own side. He trips as he steps off the curb again, rights himself with a hand against the hood of his car. Alec scoops the boomerang from the ground and waves it in Dana's face.

The man ducks into his car now, kicks up the engine, and squeals backward and away. Alec and Dana both watch the car fishtail onto the next street and disappear. The heat of the day rises up from the ground and creeps up her legs. Her knees wobble and she almost falls.

"Walk much?" Her brother sneers.

Her body stiffens, every muscle, then she reels toward him, punches his jaw, plunges her fists into his shoulder, his stomach. He topples to the ground beside the bushes, half-laughing, grabbing at her hands. She drops on top of him, hands still flailing. Finally he grasps both her wrists and stills her. His breath comes fast, and he sniffs a trickle of blood back up into his nose, pretending it's not there.

"It didn't hurt," he says. "I could hardly tell you were there." He rolls aside and stands, sloughing her off himself, letting go of her wrists last of all and leaving her behind in the dirt.

Acknowledgments

Most of us who write do so because we feel compelled to tell our stories. Finding readers usually involves exponentially more rejection than acceptance, and for every book that's published, easily ten more deserve to be as well, so I'm especially grateful and delighted to be able to share this collection with you. Thank you for reading.

Enormous gratitude to Dr. Ross Tangedal, Cornerstone Press Director & Publisher, for selecting and believing in my manuscript, and to the press editorial and design teams—Carolyn Czerwinski, Grace Dahl, Kirsten Faulkner, Hannah Fenrick, Brett Hill, Ryan Jensen, Kenzie Kierstyn, Eli Masini, Maddy Mauthe, Maggie Payson, Lauren Rudesill, Maria Scherer, Arianna Soto, Cat Scheinost, Anthony Thiel, and Chloe Verhelst—for their help in creating this book.

Deepest thanks, also, to journal editors and staff who originally recognized and/or published these stories:

"Alone," *Arts & Letters*

"Sweetness," *Prime Number Magazine*

"Next to the Fortune-Teller's House," *Stealing Time: A Literary Magazine for Parents* and *Skyline*

"Sorry Enough," *Gargoyle*;

"No Good," *Streetlight*

"Heart Blown Through," *The Petigru Review*

"Things Are Already Better Someplace Else," *The Los Angeles Review*

"The Secret Life of Otto and Hilda," *Valparaiso Fiction Review*

"Regular English," *Raleigh Review*

"Trespassing," *The Bangalore Review*

"Girl at the Gas-a-Thon," *Sequestrum*

"Everything Was the Color Red," (earlier version, titled "Stop"), *Fixional*

"Damage," *Steel Toe Review*

"Grown-Up Party," *Pithead Chapel*

*Larry Brown Short Story Award finalist

Thanks to Doug Silver who shared editorial insights on several stories in this collection.

Abundant gratitude and affection for my creative family, especially my Arma-dillhers (Sue Baller-Shepard, Teresa Burns Gunther, and Charmaine Wilkerson), Priscilla Bourgoine, Ellen Prentiss Campbell, Shelly Cato, Sharon Harrigan, Cindy House, Jocelyn Johnson, Ayesu Lartey, Kirstin-Paige Madonia, Louise Marburg, Celeste Mohammed, Betty Joyce Nash, Pam Petro, Eric Sasson, Nancy Strauss, and so many others with whom I've traded work and morale boosting over the years. Other nurturing communities I'm grateful for include Charlottesville Women Writers, the Moseley Writers Group, my Lesley University fiction MFA cohort and friends, WriterHouse, Sewanee Writers' Conference, Bread Loaf Writers' Conference, Juniper Summer Writing Institute, The Writer's Hotel, Virginia Center for the Creative Arts, Ragdale Foundation, Vermont Studio Center, and the Writers' Colony at Dairy Hollow. With special thanks to Richard Bausch, Christine Schutt, and the late Barry Hannah for their gracious support and generosity of spirit.

For friends and family who've believed in me for ages, especially Elizabeth Clark, Nagini Paravastu Dalal, Kathryn Easton, Tracy Hesler, Jane Hesler, Yana Goddard, Lindsay Lowdon, Maggie Bassen McGary, Tina Panella, Pascale Perrot, and Stacy Warner Price, and for my mother, Aimée Noonan for cheering me on since I could hold a pencil.

And most gigantic love and infinite gratitude for the unwavering, enthusiastic, loving support of my children, Clara and Jillian Hesler and my child by another mother, CJ Grooms, and for my husband Jeffrey Hesler—for all things, forever and always.

Jody Hobbs Hesler has written ever since she could hold a pencil and now lives and writes in the foothills of the Blue Ridge Mountains. Her stories and other work have appeared in *Los Angeles Review, Valparaiso Fiction Review, Necessary Fiction, CRAFT, Pithead Chapel*, and elsewhere. Growing up, she split time between suburban Richmond, Virginia, and the mountains outside Winchester, Virginia. Experiences of all three regions flavor her writing. She teaches at WriterHouse in Charlottesville, Virginia, and reads for *The Los Angeles Review*. Her debut novel, *Without You Here*, is forthcoming in November 2024.